THE REASON WHY CROWS IN AFRICAN COUNTRIES HAVE WHITE COLOR

SAINT JULIAN PRESS

Praise for – THE REASON WHY CROWS IN AFRICAN COUNTRIES HAVE WHITE COLOR

"Thanks to Sister Rosina, this marvelous collection of traditional Ghanaian stories and proverbs will intrigue you, make you smile, and prod you to think more deeply about your own life. Here is a deep well from which God's timeless wisdom can be drawn for us in our time."

—The Most Rev. Michael B. Curry
Presiding Bishop of The Episcopal Church and
author of *Love is the Way* and *Songs My Grandma Sang*

For almost 20 years, I have been finding opportunities for Rosina Ampah to tell her stories to children and adults in a wide variety of school, church, and community settings, first in Florida and later in Washington State. These events have produced a universally enthusiastic response from hosts and guests alike. The leaders with whom I coordinate her visits usually beg me to alert them whenever she is due back to their area. I have met people, especially children, who remember her stories – in detail – a year afterward. That's humbling for me, a preacher whose words are often forgotten within minutes of the time I speak to them. There is great power in the oral tradition that Rosina articulates so effectively!

—The Rev. David Mesenbring
Episcopal Priest

One may ask why the use of proverbs is so widespread in Africa. In this book, Rosina Ampah shows an indigenous people's ability to speak in symbolic language drawing from the everydayness of life. This book defies the fallacy that Africa can only be approached as a repository of rawness devoid of any conceptualization. Rosina Ampah unearths reasoning as an African art of interrogating matter in simple but crafty conveyance. Thoughtful readers will enjoy this tapestry of stories more if they open themselves up to the "reason" of things beyond their first appearances and forms.

—S. N. Nyeck, Ph.D.
Associate Professor of Africana Studies
University of Colorado, Boulder

Curious readers and lovers of folklore will delight in this unique collection of Ghanaian stories populated with talking crows, scheming spiders, and magical monkeys that open an enchanted doorway into the rich cultural realm of Ghana and its people. The wise and witty proverbs that accompany each story are best appreciated when read aloud to better hear the voice of Rosina Ampah, a gifted storyteller with a head full of wisdom and a heart full of love for the people of her native country.

—Same Chittum, Ph.D.

This book defines an amazing, hard-working, and lovely grandmother. Her interest in future generations and the need to preserve traditions compel her to chronicle the proverbs and traditional stories she heard as a child and retold time and again since then. These tales are captivating, the characters appealing, and written vividly. They recall sitting around the feet of one's grandmother, listening to stories and proverbs. This is a must-have for all.

—Dr. (Mrs.) Vivian Etsiapa Boamah

As a healthcare chaplain serving an institution in rural Western Pennsylvania, I have never resided more than 25 miles from where I now live. I have never been to Africa. Yet Rosina Ampah's telling of proverbs of Ghana, in her much anticipated second volume, resonates with me as she captures in stories of animals, fowl, and insects the essence of human nature. As I tell my patients, human nature is human nature. Rosina's stories provide lessons about who we are, what we do, and the consequences of what we do, whether we live in Ghana or anywhere in the world. Because of its universal application, it is a book for everyone.

—Monica Maghrak

Why the Crows in African Countries Have White Color instantly reminded me of *Aesop's Fables* which I read as a youth. I imagined myself back on Sr. Rosina Ampah's porch in Cape Coast, Ghana listening to this wisdom.

The stories come from a rich heritage and are a delight. They are sprinkled with humor as they evoke life lessons for all ages. These are stories meant to be shared especially read out loud in the community. We are blessed to have these proverbs, this wisdom at our fingertips.

They are a gift of wisdom from a long tradition of storytelling. "For wisdom becomes known through speech and education through the words of the tongue." — (Sirach 4:24)

—Rev. Rhonda Rogers
Episcopal Priest

THE REASON WHY CROWS

IN AFRICAN COUNTRIES

HAVE WHITE COLOR

A Book of Ghanaian Proverbs
A Remembrance and Retelling of Traditional Stories By

Reverend Canon Rosina Ampah, OSH
Order of Saint Helena

SAINT JULIAN PRESS
HOUSTON

Published by
SAINT JULIAN PRESS, Inc.
2053 Cortlandt, Suite 200
Houston, Texas 77008

www.saintjulianpress.com

ISBN-13: 978-1-955194-10-5
Library of Congress Control Number: 2022942682

Digital Cover Art: *African Pied Crow*
Cover Art & Design: Ron Starbuck

To my children
Eric Kodjo Asamoah Boateng,
Ekua Ata Panyin, and Kakra.

PROVERBS 4:5-7 (NRSVA)

5 Get wisdom; get insight: do not forget, nor turn away
from the words of my mouth.

6 Do not forsake her, and she will keep you;
love her, and she will guard you.

7 The beginning of wisdom is this: Get wisdom,
and whatever else you get, get insight.

CONTENTS

PREFACE

This book of Ghanaian proverbs is written in memory of the late Mr. Kwame Ampah-Kuma of Krofuw in the Central Region of Ghana. He was my grandfather and the Grand Master of Proverbs in the place where I grew up.

Basically, Ghanaians are highly idiomatic people. Children are taught in proverbs and wise sayings when they are growing up. Every family knows how to convey messages to children or relatives through proverbs and stories, more so than most cultures I have known.

The proverbs written in this book were drawn from memory when I decided to record some of these treasures for future generations as well as for others outside the Ghanaian culture who may be interested in learning about the wisdom within these proverbs. I felt that with the fast-changing world, children growing up later may not have the chance to hear such proverbs and learn from the rich treasure within their culture. I count myself lucky to have lived in several different areas of Ghana as well as with several different members of my family. I also lived with friends of my parents at different times when I was growing up.

In the way Ghanaian culture is set up, one must be equipped with the gift of understanding these wise sayings, the proverbs, and the stories, or one would miss a great deal of communication. Linguists are trained in special ways with skills for understanding the meaning hidden within the proverbs and the sayings to be the communicating link between the people and the Ohen (Chief or King) or Ohenbaa (Queen). This is so, so that the King or the Queen does not have to deal directly with the people.

Secondly, proverbs are important because one can say a lot in two or three proverbs. For example, if a parent or somebody says to you: "Mfeda muhunii, ne epe wombo!"—meaning what I saw last year must not be seen again, or you must be careful so that what happened to you last year must not be repeated—and you are well equipped in understanding proverbs, your immediate reaction would be to stop and look again at what you are doing because this specific proverb is a signal for warning. Whoever uses the proverb is reminding the hearer about an incident that may have happened in the past and should not be repeated since the event was not pleasant or was not a good experience.

In general, people are aware of what is around them because of the repeated proverbs and stories that go along with what happens, even though it may have been years since the actual incident took place. I share this treasure with the hope that the people who read them may find them to be treasures too.

Reverend Canon Rosina Ampah, OSH
Order of Saint Helena

INTRODUCTION
BY MR. S. K. AMPAH

This little book of Akan proverbs written by a Ghanaian woman is an attempt to a great work. To know and understand the meaning of proverbs in a speech declares one to be a possessor of intelligence and much wisdom. Thus, to be able to use them oneself in speech shows that one is a born philosopher of much understanding. It is not found as a common gift among men in Ghana, much less women. Therefore, for a woman to author a book of some length on proverbs with their meanings in literal English is an unusual attempt of a unique woman.

In the case of the author of this present book, one who knows the background of her life, her antecedents and family lineage, as well as her birthplace, and the genealogy of the paternal and maternal line of her predecessors may attribute the gift to inheritance or talent. But it takes interest to be able to produce what one has gathered up in him or herself from his or her youth. "God moves in a mysterious way, his wonders to perform," says William Cowper's hymn.

The author or writer of this book of Akan proverbs is the daughter of this introducer, but though he has been born with this talent, he has never written one proverb down for publishing; neither has any of his ancestors dreamed of such a thing. Yet the author's grandfather, who was my father, was a Grand-Master in these Akan proverbs and maxims, so much so that he could not speak anywhere, in public or in private, without using a proverb straight away.

In Akan Native Courts, people are not allowed to use proverbs in their speech before the court, but my father always asked for permission to use them; otherwise, he must not be asked to speak at all. There is therefore no doubt that this young woman must have inherited this gift from her grandsire, whom she knew when she was noticeably young and only for a few years.

Ghanaian proverbs may be divided into three grades or kinds:

1. Proverbs used in speech.

2. Proverbs used by Drummers to inform people at distances what is happening at certain places.

3. Proverbs by the Chief's Horn-Blowers, in praise of Chiefs and other people of rank and position.

Also, two Drummers of different Asafo Companies (Local Warriors) can ask and answer questions of each other by drums.

Sister Rosina's book, though confined to spoken proverbs alone, is an honorable attempt to aggregate complete books of this type, which may include some of the above areas. Therefore, it is fervently hoped that many readers of the book, especially Akan readers, and Ghanaians in general, may be moved as aforesaid to soon follow with bigger volumes of Akan proverbs consisting of all the different grades and kinds of Akan proverbs, maxims, and other customary rites. We need to sustain interest in this art, which is gradually dwindling into extinction. I am afraid that rising generations are growing more and more ignorant of this rich heritage.

S. K. Ampah

THE REASON WHY CROWS IN AFRICAN COUNTRIES HAVE WHITE COLOR

THE REASON WHY CROWS IN AFRICAN COUNTRIES HAVE WHITE COLOR

Many, many years ago, African crows did not have the white neck as they do today. This story reveals how African crows got their white neck color.

Once upon a time, there lived in a certain village a woman named Baawa, who had an only daughter named Ekua. Ekua decided to go snail hunting with her friends, who were going into a nearby forest in search of snails. To get to the forest, they had to cross a large river, and the river's name was Atta.

When the girls reached the edge of the River Atta, before they could cross the river, each girl had to promise the River Atta that she would give him three snails if he would let her cross safely to the other side. The river would then open the way for the girl to pass. So, they each made a promise and crossed over. When it came to Madam Baawa's daughter Ekua, she also made the same promise, and the river opened the way for her to pass.

All the girls went into the forest and searched for snails, but since that was Ekua's first time, as luck would have it, she did not find any snails. When the girls returned in the evening and wanted to cross the River Atta again to return home, each girl offered what she had promised, except Ekua, who could not because she did not find any snails. So as soon as she stepped into the river to cross, she started sinking slowly to the bottom of the large river. So, she quickly began singing the following message to her mother through the girls. Her message was to go and tell her mother to bring some drinks and eggs to redeem her before the River Atta swallowed her up:

Those who are going,
Those who are going,
When you go, tell my mother
To bring nine bottles of liquor
Tell her to also bring nine eggs
To redeem me from the River Atta
The River Atta is taking me away!!

So, the girls ran as fast as they could and went straight to Ekua's mother to deliver her message. Madam Baawa quickly went and bought the drinks and the eggs and set off towards the River Atta as fast as her legs could carry her. She had not gone far when she met the vulture on the outskirts of the town. The vulture asked Madam Baawa where she was going, that she seemed to be in such a hurry. Madam Baawa explained to the vulture what had happened, and that she was going to redeem her daughter Ekua from the River Atta, who had taken her captive. The vulture asked Madam Baawa if it was all right to accompany her. Madam Baawa said it was all right to have company, so the vulture followed her.

A little further along, she met the crow, who also asked Madam Baawa and the vulture where they were going in such a hurry. Madame Baawa repeated her sad news to the crow, and the crow decided to accompany them. So, the three of them went together until they reached the banks of the River Atta. Upon their arrival, Madam Baawa saw only the head and shoulders of her daughter, because she had sunk down that much into the river. Madam Baawa quickly put the eggs into the river, poured the drinks into the river, and pleaded with the river god to release her only daughter Ekua.

The vulture asked if it was all right to sing, and Madam Baawa thought the vulture was offering something to help her daughter come out from the river, so she answered yes. But instead, the vulture started singing the following song that would push the girl deeper into the river:

Futur, futur push her down!
Large river push her down!
Futur, futur push her down!
Large river push her down!

Suddenly, Madam Baawa realized that the vulture was asking the River Atta to drag her daughter down and that she was sinking faster. She quickly grabbed the vulture's mouth and said, "No more of your songs, you wicked vulture."

The crow immediately picked up a song without permission or warning:

My mother's only daughter Ekua is sinking!
Give her back to me; she is the only one I have!
My mother's only daughter Ekua is sinking!
Give her back to me; she is the only one I have!

As soon as the crow sang the song, Ekua started rising from the water, the crow continued to sing, and Ekua continued to come up. Without warning, the vulture got loose and started singing its negative song, and Ekua began to go down again. So, Madam Baawa caught it again by the mouth and told crow that she was leaving the scene with the vulture until Ekua was completely out of the river. Madam Baawa asked the crow to bring Ekua along when she was released from the river. So the crow kept singing until Ekua walked out of the river to safety. Madam Baawa returned with the vulture as soon as Ekua was out of danger. Madam Baawa asked both the crow and the vulture to join her and her daughter at their home because she wanted to honor both for accompanying her to rescue Ekua from the river.

When they reached Madam Baawa's house, she gave the crow a white cloth and a beautiful blue-black silk cloth to reward its kindness. Madam Baawa then gave the vulture a dirty grey cloth and told it that it was because of its cruel attitude toward her and her daughter. She also told the vulture that it would always search through garbage to feed, and dead animals would be its food forever. She then told the crow, to tie the white cloth around its neck as a symbol of victory so that people would see how pretty it looks, so it did.

That is why African crows have beautiful blue-black silk and a white neck color and sing out Madam Baawa's name when you ask them how they got the white color. The response is always the same: *Baawa, Baawa, Baawa!* The crows mean it was a gift from

Madame Baawa.

In this story, Ekua copied what her friends were doing without knowing the consequences of the promise she made to the River Atta, which almost led to her death. Many young people sometimes follow their friends blindly, not knowing what they are getting themselves into. By the time they realize it, things have already gone bad. And so the following proverbs tell us something about that. There are many lessons to be learned from the above story from several points of view: Why the other girls did not give Ekua some of their snails so she could pass through the water is a lesson to be explored.

A proverb or wise saying to go with such a story would be:

If one is too impatient to wait for the food to cook, one always ends up with uncooked food!

When a child takes a lump of food, they must take what they can chew easily.

If a child has a large mouth, they blow a horn with it, not a mortar.

When you want to meddle in other people's affairs, do it closer to home, not in a foreign country.

If a person is smart, they must tackle what they can succeed at, not something impossible.

If you do not know what dying is, just look at sleep!

A child cracks a snail but not a tortoise!

If a child decides to try a new hairstyle, you cut it for them and let them look at themselves.

THE REASON WHY MR. SPIDER HAS A BALD HEAD

Many centuries ago, Mr. Spider had an exceptionally fine head of hair like everyone else. Until one day, an incident happened through his fault that rendered him bald for the rest of his life. Following is the story of what happened to Mr. Spider's hair.

In ancient times, many people did not eat when they lost someone to death, especially when that person was very dear to them. However, they made an exception to this rule: people would feed their guests and strangers from out of town, so they would not faint on their return journey home. When Mr. Spider's mother-in-law had a death in the family, he had to attend a funeral in his mother-in-law's hometown, and he did. When the time came to feed the guests, Mr. Spider refused and would not accept the offer to feed himself.

Well, as time went on, the family tried again and again, but Mr. Spider refused to eat anything, so they left him alone. On the second day, Mr. Spider was very hungry but still did not want to ask his relatives to provide something for him to eat. Instead, he went through the kitchen area to see what was available but could find nothing. When he walked past the kitchen area again, he smelled cooked beans, so he waited for a while and went into the kitchen to see who was there, but found nobody.

Mr. Spider then took his hat and put some hot beans into it. As soon as he did that, his mother-in-law opened the inner chamber door to come out. Mr. Spider quickly put his hat back on his head with the hot beans in it and lied to his mother-in-law, saying that he had come to say goodbye to her because he was leaving town. Unfortunately, his mother-in-law decided that she had not had a chance to visit with him, so she said that she would like to walk halfway with him so they could visit. Mr. Spider was in real trouble; even though the top of his head was burning, there was no way he wanted to disgrace himself in front of his mother-in-law by taking off his hat because he had the hot stolen beans in it. So he decided to trick her with a song. Following is the song he sang:

My in-law, you can leave me here! You can leave me here!

Someone should go and see my own village where they are shaking
   their hats!

Wonyo! Wonyo! They are shaking their hats. Wonyo! Wonyo!

As Mr. Spider sang, wonyo, wonyo, he shook his own head around just to shake the burning sensation on top of his head around for some relief. But his mother-in-law wanted to continue to visit since she did not see him that often. So they walked on together, and Mr. Spider continued to ask the in-law to leave and shook his head for some relief as he sang. By the time his mother-in-law finally left him, and Mr. Spider was finally able to take off his hat, his head was all burned because the hot beans had cooked his skin. It took so long to get better, that by the time Mr. Spider's burns were healed, he had a huge scar on his scalp, and no hair would grow on his head again. That is why Mr. Spider is bald up to this day!

A story like this would be told to teach how one must be honest and not pretend to handle what they know they cannot. Because if Mr. Spider had not followed the custom blindly and lied to himself, he would not have gotten into a situation where he had to steal and suffer in the end. My parents/family told me to tell the truth, no matter what it was, and not lie. Since when you lie, you must keep lying to cover it up! Dishonesty always leads people to disgrace, according to the moral of this story. The wise sayings and proverbs that go with a story like this would be the following:

Do what is good for you and not what fashion dictates!

Tell the truth and shame the devil.

Wicked deeds always come out.

You end up breaking her pot when you become too shy around your mother-in-law!

When one tries to get away from stepping in the mud, they sometimes end up falling into it!

When the goat was rubbing its dirty body on the owner's beautiful home, it thought it was spoiling the house for him; but by the time it finished, its own skin was peeled off!

WHY CHIPMUNKS HAVE THE LINES ON THEIR BODIES

Once upon a time, many animals lived together as one family. They shared things in common and were incredibly happy until the following incident happened and made them go their separate ways.

During one bitter harmattan season, all of the animals' bodies were dried up and looked so pale that they decided to make palm kernel oil to use when they showered to keep their bodies from drying up. All the animals worked for weeks to collect and crack kernels. They fried the kernels and got plenty of oil. After the oil was ready, they poured it into a big basin and put it outside on a table to cool off while they went about their daily business.

Each animal went out for the day to find food or perform some task for the good of the community. The chipmunk came home earlier than expected while the rest were still out, and was going about his chores in the house when he accidentally bumped into the table that held the oil and overturned the basin. Every drop of the oil in the basin was lost. You can imagine chipmunk's horror when this happened! He wondered why this should happen to him instead of the other animals. He started weeping immediately, went out, and sat by the main gate, waiting for the rest of the animals to return home.

He knew how many weeks it took them to collect the kernels and crack them to make the oil, and now it was all gone!

As the animals came back home, he sang to them what had happened and how he was afraid to face the tiger with this information. The cat was the first to come home, and when he heard the song from the chipmunk, he said that he was just a small boy, so chipmunk should wait for the tiger himself.

Following was the song sung by the chipmunk as the animals came home one by one:

I have overturned the oil of all the animals!
Response: Senkyiren

I have overturned the oil of all the animals!

Response: Senkyiren

The tears that I am sharing

Response: Senkyiren

It makes me incredibly sad

Response: Senkyiren

Because I am afraid of the tiger

Response: Senkyiren!

As the larger animals approached home, they saw chipmunk sitting by the main gate weeping, so they asked what the matter with him was. He started to sing his song repeatedly, and they were very sorry for him and said, it is all right with us, but you will have to wait for the tiger and see what he will say. In the late evening, the tiger was seen coming home, and the chipmunk started his song again. When the tiger reached where chipmunk was, he noticed that he was weeping and asked him what was the matter? The chipmunk sang the song again and the tiger said to him in a loud voice, "This was for one of my ears, so I need to hear the song again."

The chipmunk knew he was in trouble, so, as he began to sing the song again, he started looking for a place to hide. As soon as the song was over, the tiger reached out to grab the chipmunk, but he was too fast for him. And so the tiger's nails scratched the back of the chipmunk and gave him the perpetual marks that we see on chipmunks today.

Even though these stories are about animals, their characters show us how difficult it is to try to live in harmony with everyone. A story like this will teach us how to be careful when one lives with many different individuals because you never know what may offend anyone.

A proverb or wise sayings that follow a story like this would be:

When a family member turns against you, it is harder than an outsider.

The fox and chicken do not sleep together.

No matter how beautiful the hen dances, it never pleases the hawk.

If your enemy tries to imitate your dance, they always twist their waist!

Hatred has no medicine!

No matter how beautiful the cockroach dances, it does not please the chicken!

THE REASON WHY CATS LIKE TO SLAP DOGS

An awfully long time ago, in a certain village lived a poor hunter and his parents. The family's small possessions included a cat and a dog. They were so poor and unskilled that their only means of survival were tilling the land or hunting. They depended upon what the land yielded them in return for their hard labor. However, one of their sons was a skillful hunter who would occasionally bring game home from his hard hunt and support them with meat for their meals.

One day as they were working together on their new farmland, one of the sons found an old ring in the soil. He quickly picked it up and went down to the little brook that runs by their plot to clean it. He thought it might be a good sell so they could buy some nice food for themselves. He did not know that what he had discovered in the soil was a magic ring that would forever change their lives and the lives of everyone in their village. After he reached the brook, he stooped down and washed the mud out of the ring, but the ring was not getting cleaned. So, he decided to rub it against the stone to see if that would help to shine it. When the ring touched the stone, a genie appeared and scared him half to death!

The genie said, "I am at your service. What do you need?" In his panic, the young man said, I need food. In an instant, food of all kinds appeared, enough for several people to have many meals out of it.

The young man dismissed the genie and called his family to come and see what God had given them. They could not believe their eyes! They thought at first that he found the food there and were afraid to go closer in case they were being lured into a trap, until he told them where it came from.

They were so happy that they could hardly eat the food set before them; they wanted to see if that was not just a one-time trick. So, he demonstrated the ring again by rubbing it against the stone and, in an instant, saw the genie appear with the statement: At your service. The young man then asked him to bring them some new clothes, which was done immediately. You can imagine how happy they were! I bet they had never been so happy in their lives as when they saw the beautiful new clothes and food waiting for them at the brookside. They ate, later washed, and put on their new clothes, which perfectly fit them.

The young man quickly realized the power of what he had in his hand and took advantage of it as soon as they came home from the farm that evening. Extremely late in the night, when people had retired to their beds, he ordered the genie to build houses for each of his brothers and one larger one for his parents. He asked for two buildings, one for guests and one for himself. Within a few hours, everything was in place. So in the morning, you can imagine how people were flocking in from everywhere to come and see this miracle of overnight houses. The question was: How could homes appear overnight with such complicated architectural designs? People felt as though, they were just dreaming, and that the places would disappear as soon as they closed their eyes again! People were attracted to the mysterious buildings but, at the same time, afraid of what the houses might mean to the whole village in the end. The family's status soon became the talk of the village; how did they come by such riches? However, the family members were good people, so they decided to share their good fortune with the whole village.

The young man explained everything to Chief Kweku Ababio,

chief of the village where he had gotten his good fortune, and said he would be willing to help develop their town. The chief's palace was the next to be called into place, and soon the people were eager for theirs to be called too. After everything was in place, the village looked like a dreamland out of nowhere. The chief quickly promoted the young man to join the village counselors and planners, so he could oversee what needed to be accomplished. Within a month, the genie had called into being a whole new village—not a simple village anymore but a little paradise. Everything you can think of was there; people had good, beautiful new houses to live in, which cost them practically nothing. The lucky family was looked upon like gods incarnate.

Not long after this good fortune, their father died and was buried in a beautiful tomb outside his house. Time passed, and years after his father's death, the young man said to his mother that he wanted a wife and that he wanted to marry the princess of the next town. His mother objected to her son's idea of marrying the princess of the next city because it was very risky for him to go that far, knowing that he was not a prince. However, his mother agreed with him that he needed a wife.

He told his mother that he had fallen in love with the princess as soon as he met her years ago when they were just youngsters. However, they were so poor that he did not think she would marry him. But now, nothing would stop him from marrying her if she wanted him as a husband. Even though his mother begged him not to pursue the marriage with the princess, the young man put his words into action. He sent some Elders from his town into the king's house to ask for the hand of his daughter in marriage. The king was surprised but respected his request and consulted with his wife and later with the princess herself. The princess agreed to marry him, so permission was sent to him that if he could provide all the requirements befitting a princess, he would be welcome to marry her.

That was not a big deal with the genie around. Everything that custom required, he gave double, and within a few weeks from the day he received the consent, he had finished every customary rite and was ready for his wife. You can imagine what a home the princess came into! She had never seen any place like it before; his father's house compared to her new home was nothing! She had maids to wait on her, butlers to take care of all her needs, and everything a woman would hope for in the house. She did not have to do anything if she so desired except to be with the man she loved. The young man built extra houses for all the attendants in the big house area, including some for the musicians whose job was to play music all the time to entertain their guests.

As for the wedding itself, you have never seen anything like it, nor would I be able to describe to you its splendor! People were so happy for them because they seemed to be so much in love with each other. Furthermore, nobody had ever seen such beauty and splendor or would ever see its equal again in their lifetime; everything was exactly right and perfect! There was happiness everywhere, except for the groom's mother, who was still so afraid of her son's future that she could not bring herself to enjoy the celebration. The news of their wedding spread like wildfire worldwide, and people came to visit them to see for themselves what they had heard through rumors. Unfortunately, the news reached the ears of an evil, wicked magician in a distant country who immediately knew the source of the couple's riches.

Since he was that evil, he could not see others being that happy, so he decided to put an end to the young man's popularity by coming to steal the ring from him. He said to himself: I will let him suffer for claiming such fame within such a short time and for having the nerve to marry the beautiful princess.

On the other hand, the couple were incredibly happy with each other and were content to enjoy their riches. Everyone in the family was content, except once again his mother, who still worried about her son's choice of a wife. Other than that, she, too, was delighted and content to see her family happy.

In the meantime, the wicked magician from the distant country was seriously at work on how to steal the ring from the young man. He collected magical herbs, brewed them into magical lotions, and gave them to one of his servants to travel into the young man's country. He instructed his servant to pretend to be selling some magical lotions when he came around the couple's house, and someone would call him into the house to look at them. As soon as he entered the house, he should spray the house with the magical powder he had hidden in his lotions, and everyone would fall asleep. He should go directly into the couple's bedroom, and he would find a small bag hanging on one of the bedposts. The ring would be in that bag; he should take it out and leave the palace as quickly as possible. The servant did as his master had instructed him, and sure enough, he was called into the house by one of the maids, who thought her mistress would like to see some of the body lotions.

As soon as he entered the building, he sprayed all the people into sleep and went straight into the bedroom, where he saw the bag as his master had predicted. He investigated the bag and found the ring, then sneaked out of the house as quickly as possible without anybody seeing him. He walked a little distance from the home and rubbed the ring against a stone. The genie appeared with the same words: "I am at your service." The wicked servant instructed the genie as his master had told him, to remove all the man's possessions, including his dog and cat, from their beautiful palace and to carry the princess and everything else into the magician's village in the far away country.

Within a second, the palace, with all its music and happiness, vanished as quickly as it had appeared months ago; everything was gone! It did not take long for neighbors to notice the disappearance of the palace from the town. So the man was summoned home from a town meeting to witness what had happened. At first, the man thought his wife might have been playing with the ring and got the genie to take her away somewhere and did not know how to get herself back home. But as time passed, he became afraid of what might have happened and the town with him. The chief of his village and the king of the next village sent warriors and search parties to search far and wide for her and the house, but they did not find the princess or the house anywhere. You can imagine the man's pain and the sorrow of the man's mother, who all along had not been having good feelings about the marriage. The blow came when the king told the man that if, within three months, he did not bring his daughter back, safe and sound, he would execute him!

The man was so brokenhearted and sad about his wife's disappearance that he did not care to live anyway. He prayed for death many times, but death would not take him. His brothers and friends tried to help him by setting up their own search parties, but they could not find any helpful information for him either. Unfortunately, time was not waiting for him either. As days turned into weeks and weeks into months, it became definite that he would have to die by the executioner's knife. Of course, he felt this to be true with all his heart: that he would gladly die rather than live without knowing his wife's whereabouts for the rest of his life. Death was far much better!

On the other hand, the wicked magician had a house in a very remote village in the country where he lived, and one had to cross a vast river to get to his island village. The house had become so dirty with medicines and animal blood that you would not believe if you had seen it that it was the same house taken from the town less than three months ago. The magician did not care for the princess, her attendants, or whoever else was in the house, so he left them alone in their sorrow to keep each other company; knowing they would never see their families again was enough for his fancy. However, the maids tried to comfort their mistress, telling her that her husband would come and rescue her from that miserable place as soon as he got home.

The magician built a huge wooden box, with smaller ones to fit inside each larger one until he got the smallest box, to seal it off as a huge block; he put the ring inside it, locked the door to the room that contained the box and threw the key to the lock into the river.

He reasoned with himself that no one would find the key to that room even if he died. Furthermore, he thought that if even someone could break into the room, they could not reach the center of that vast sealed wooden box to find the magic ring.

Now the miserable husband had only two more weeks to find his wife or die by execution, which he was looking forward to gladly. He woke up every morning wondering why he was still alive, but that morning when he woke up, his cat came and jumped onto his lap, something the cat had never done before. She started rubbing herself on his body, so he asked, What is the matter with you? Are you hungry or sad because I am about to die? To his total surprise and astonishment, the cat answered, Yes, I am very worried about you, so the dog and I have decided to help you. However, the road is long and the journey difficult; please advise the dog not to stop for any bones on the road as we travel.

Somehow the cat knew that the magician was aware that they would be coming to his village. So he had cooked enticing bones for the dog and lovely meat for the cat to delay them on their journey by tempting them to stop and eat, making them sleepy. However, the cat knew she would not be tempted but was worried about the dog, because he did not have self-control over his appetite for bones. Anyhow, the husband did not pin his hopes upon the adventures of the cat and dog into the unknown. The cat and the dog said goodbye to their master and embarked on their arduous journey, traveling day and night until they reached the banks of the vast river. We all know that a cat does not swim, so the dog had to carry the cat across to the other side of the river.

As soon as they walked from the banks of the river, bones and meat were everywhere, and the smell was irresistible! This was to distract them from their serious trip. The cat's tail was high in the air, and she kept going, but the dog could not resist the bones after passing a few. So he settled down to eat, even though the cat kept reminding him of their master's situation and how little time he had left. The cat went on alone, leaving the dog behind until she came and stood before a vast, tall gate. There was no way the cat could climb it, so she waited patiently. Fortunately, it was not long before someone came out of the house and the cat slipped into the building as soon as the gate was opened. She went straight into the room where the box that held the ring was and sat there thinking what to do next.

As she sat there, a huge mouse appeared and slipped into the corner to eat, but the cat did not mind it, so the mouse went and came back with several others; still, the cat did not mind them. Suddenly they all disappeared; they went and told their chief their story of a cat who would not catch them, but he did not believe their story. So they invited him to come and see for himself, and so their chief came back with them to see the cat who would not catch mice. As soon as the mice appeared with their chief, the cat grabbed the chief's neck and held him to the ground. The mice screamed and begged the cat to let their chief go, but the cat said, If you do what I tell you, he will go unharmed. If not, then I will kill him.

They all answered with one accord: We will do whatever you ask! The cat told them to chew the wooden box and make a small passage hole until they could reach the ring in the center and bring it out of the box. If they did that, their chief would go free. You can imagine the speed with which they worked! Within an hour or so, the ring was in the mouth of the smallest mouse heading toward the cat. The cat took the ring, thanked them, and released their chief unharmed as she had promised them, so they thanked the cat and went away with their chief. The cat put the ring on her claw nail and closed her paw so the ring would be secured. She went and waited by the gate as she did in the morning when she was going in. It took a long time before somebody went out of the house again, and she was able to slip out.

As soon as she was out of the house, she headed back on her homeward journey with great speed. The dog had been eating and sleeping until he saw the cat coming from the village so fast that he got up and followed her, thinking that someone was chasing the cat. When he caught up with the cat, he asked the cat if she had found the ring, but the cat did not mind him at first until they reached the bank of the river. The dog asked again if the cat had found the ring and said that if the cat was not going to talk to him, then he would not take her across the river. So, she was forced to say that she had found the ring.

The dog then said to the cat that he was the senior, so he must keep the ring, or they will not go across the river; the cat, being aware of the time factor, gave the ring to the dog. The dog put the ring into his mouth and began carrying the cat across to the other side of the river; the dog, being full of all those good bones, was very thirsty. So he opened his mouth to drink some water, forgetting the ring in his mouth, and out went the ring into the river! Immediately, a medium-sized fish came and swallowed it. That same day, another bigger fish swallowed the fish that had swallowed the ring, and the following day a huge fish swallowed the second fish that had swallowed the first fish with the ring in its belly.

Meanwhile, the dog never said anything to the cat, so they both journeyed home with great speed. They arrived home three days before the execution day. As soon as their master saw them, he regained hope and asked: Did you find the ring? The cat answered, Yes, but it is with the dog. However, when the master asked the dog to give him the ring, he could not say a word or produce the ring. The cat was so infuriated by the dog's silence that she jumped on him and started slapping him, scratching him until he admitted that the ring fell into the river when he opened his mouth to drink. The cat then asked, Why did you not tell me before we made this long journey home? Without waiting for an answer, she dashed out again without the dog on her way back to the riverbank.

The cat's tail was like a flag in the air as she sped into the coming night! By noon the next day, she was already by the bank of the vast river. The cat sat motionlessly and waited. After a few minutes, a group of small fish started swimming toward the bank of the river; the cat caught a couple and put them on her claws, then put her paw in the river and waited. As luck would have it, she did not have to wait for long. A colossal fish came dashing from the river, ready to eat the small fish from the cat's paws, but the cat was ready for it; she quickly put her paws into its mouth and threw it ashore, and grabbed its neck.

The big fish begged to be put back into the water before it died, but the cat said, throw up the fish you swallowed this morning, and you will go free. The fish obeyed and threw up the fish. Then the cat grabbed that one while she threw the big one back into the river. She told the medium fish to throw up the smaller fish it swallowed yesterday, and that it would go free if it did. The fish did as she had directed it. Then the cat did the same with the small fish, only this time the cat said to the fish: Throw up the ring you swallowed yesterday morning, and you will also go free, and so the fish did and was set free.

As soon as the cat got the ring and threw the small fish back into the river, she started her homeward journey. She did not stop running until she reached her master's house. It was about four in the morning, the same morning that her master would have been executed. Her master jumped up with joy when he saw the cat was back and asked, Did you find any luck? In answer to the question, the cat put the ring into her master's hand. He quickly rubbed the ring against a stone, and immediately the genie appeared with the same words as usual: I am at your service.

The man quickly ordered the genie to bring back the house and its contents, except to remove any foreign inclusions that may have been added. Within a second, the house, filthy as it was, was back in its original place, with its music still playing as suddenly as it had disappeared on that fateful day. The man went first into the bedroom to make sure his wife was still there, and sure enough, she was there. She was as beautiful as ever, sleeping with profound sorrow on her face. The man did not disturb her sleep but waited until she woke up in the morning. He told her that her father wanted to see her so much that she must be ready for someone to accompany her to her father's house.

On the other hand, the town was once again awakened with music that they had not heard since the disappearance of the palace. So people started running toward the palace again as though they were in a dreamland. They realized how much they had missed the music from the palace, and very soon, the news reached the king in the next town that his daughter was back again, along with the house and all its contents. Some folks even thought, the princess herself may have put her husband to that extreme test.

However, the husband produced the most elegant and expensive dresses for his wife to wear and gave her quantities of clothing and wealth before sending her to her parent's house for the visit. She dressed in her new expensive dresses and was ready for the visit with her parents, not knowing it was the end of her loving marriage until she reached home. She learned what her husband had gone through, including her own father planning to take his life that very morning if it had not been for the cat. So, her husband had informed the Elders who accompanied her to her parent's home to tell her father to keep his daughter because the young man did not know what misfortune might happen again and that he might have to die since he had no control over his destiny.

The king tried to pretend that he was just joking about the

execution to make the young man serious in the search for his daughter. Still, everyone including the Elders, knew that he was profoundly serious and would have killed him if God had not intervened and saved the young man's life. The princess mourned for her husband for the rest of her life. On the other hand, the man thanked his mother for her love and constant advice; it seemed that the young man finally understood why his mother was uncomfortable about his marrying the princess.

As for the wicked magician and his servants, the man ordered the genie to bind them and throw them to the bottom of the sea so they would not hurt other innocent people. Then the man turned to the cat and said, You were the one who saved my life and the lives of all the people I love, so you will always occupy the best place in the house. You can choose to sleep in the softest, most cozy areas if you want, including my own bed. But to the dog, he said, Because of your uncaring attitude toward my needs, especially at a crucial time in my life, you will spend the rest of your life watching over the safety of my life. You will guard my house whether I am home or away and give a warning when you see a stranger approaching my house. You will sleep outside from this day onward, and you will always be appeased with a piece of bone for your work. Despite all that punishment, the cat was still mad with the dog for doing what he did when their master was in trouble and for making her do extra work because she could not swim. That is why dogs and cats still fight up to this day.

The truth of the story was that the princess was gone for less than six months, but to those who loved her, it seemed like years. So, remember how painful it is for your loved ones when you decide to stay away intentionally without letting them know where you are. From this story, we have a lot to learn about how the kindness and caring of others help us in times of need; how the people in the town rallied around the young man and his family during their ordeal.

The proverbs that go with such a story would be:

Hastily acquired, hastily lost!

He who refuses to listen to the advice of the Elders ends up in trouble!

Help comes from where we least expect it.

Necessity is the mother of invention.

One never knows what will happen if only you are still alive.

Love and kindness are what one builds a town with!

Stubbornness does not leave a person in good places!

One reaps what one sows.

One discovers their real friends when they are in trouble.

Those who shared real tears with you are the ones who know you.

THE WOMAN AND THE ELF

There lived in a certain village many, many years ago, a hard-working couple who were farmers. They worked so efficiently on their farm that they found favor with the rest of the villagers and earned the title "chief farmers." Not only were they loved by people, but unusual as it may be, an elf fell in love with them because of their hard-working attitude and befriended them without their knowledge.

As time passed, they decided to raise a family, so the wife became pregnant, and an unbelievably beautiful daughter was born to them. The wife had to stay home and nurse the child while her husband worked alone on the farm until the baby was three months old. She returned to the farm to work again with her husband after the third month. At the farm, the woman would put her sleeping baby in a wooden tray-like bed and leave her underneath a massive tree in the shade where the couple had created their resting place while they worked in the sun.

The baby would sleep for hours and allowed her parents to work for long hours, so they thought they were lucky to be blessed with an unusual sleeping baby. The baby never cried to disturb their work while on the farm until they were ready to take a break or to eat. Nobody knew that it was a friendly elf who had been caring for their baby while they worked. The elf liked them and wanted to help them so that they could work and get enough money from their crops to care for their baby and themselves.

The couple assumed they had been blessed with a nice baby girl who could sleep for hours. It never entered their mind that there must be something odd about how their daughter slept; moreover, to have dreamt that a friendly elf would babysit for them while they struggled in the sun.

The elf would sing and swing the baby back and forth until the elf saw the couple coming when he would escape into the woods. The elf loved to watch from the shadows of the bushes the satisfaction on the parents' faces while they played with their baby after finishing their work for the day.

Following is the song sung by the elf while babysitting for the couple:

Elf: Me nye wo rogor yi asem bi aba?
Me nye wo rogor yi asem bi aba?
Adasa woye mekyire!
Me nye wo rogor yi asem bi aba?

English:
Has anything gone wrong while I am playing with you?
Has anything gone wrong while I am playing with you?
Human beings like to control every situation!
Has anything gone wrong while I am playing with you?

The elf sang the song over and over until the baby fell asleep. This babysitting went on for several months and helped the couple to continue steadily with their farm work because their baby did not interrupt the speed with which they did their work.

However, an unfortunate disaster happened to the hardworking couple when their hunter friend decided one day to pay them a visit on their farm while he was passing close by their area. On his way to their farm, he was attracted to the shady tree by a song and thinking that his friend's wife might be playing with their baby, he decided to stop there first to chat with her before going on to see the friend himself. When the hunter got closer, to his astonishment, he saw an elf swinging the baby back and forth while he sang the above beautiful song to keep the baby from crying. He watched them for a long period of time before he called the couple's name out aloud, and as soon as he did that, the elf put the baby down and disappeared.

The couple responded from inside the farm and came to their resting place, under the big shady tree. The hunter told the couple about the strange scene he had witnessed with their baby. The couple immediately realized that the elf may have been the reason their baby had not been crying. But the hunter persuaded them that it was not safe for them to be in such an area with their baby until the elf had been killed because the elf may eventually steal their baby away.

The hunter offered to assist them in killing the elf if they would cooperate with him. So, a plan was set for the following day: the couple would leave their baby as usual underneath the big tree when they came to the farm. The hunter would then go and hide where he was that afternoon while the couple pretended to work as usual. They would then come back to join the hunter to watch for the elf until he came to pick up the baby.

Somehow, it did not occur to them that the elf might listen to their plans. Furthermore, it never occurred to them that they might be planning the child's death instead of the elf's. Anyway, they ceased working for the day and went home still worried about their baby in case anything went wrong. The following day, they came to the farm to put into action what they had planned the previous day, which was to kill the elf. Consequently, they left the baby sleeping in her usual place and left, pretending to go and work as arranged. The elf came as usual and started to play with the baby when the baby was left alone. He sang the same song to her when she began to cry. The elf carried the baby in his arms and started swinging her back and forth, singing:

Me nye wo rogor yi asem bi aba?
Me nye wo rogor yi asem bi aba?
Adasa woye mekyire mekyire!
Me nye wo rogor yi asem bi aba?

The sad part of the story is that the people did not even pay the slightest attention to what the elf was saying, or they would not have done what they did. However, as soon as the couple joined the hunter and the elf's back was turned toward the group, the hunter took good aim at the elf and fired his gun. But as soon as the bullet was let loose, the elf turned around, received the bullet with the baby, put her down, and disappeared into the woods.

The baby's mother started screaming and wailing while she ran to the spot where her baby was lying, and found her dead. She was beside herself with grief as they carried the dead baby home, wailing as they went. People gathered around them as soon as they reached the village, asking questions about how this had happened to them. After they narrated their story, the villagers blamed them for their ingratitude toward the elf who had helped them to work on their farm.

They were also blamed for their stupidity in listening to the evil plot of the hunter who called himself their friend. Furthermore, the wise Elders of the village asked the hunter to tell them the song the elf sang. After listening to the words, they asked the hunter and the couple if they had paid any attention to the words of the elf's song. They answered no.

The Elders explained that the elf was asking "if any harm had happened while he and the baby played together?" The truth was that nothing would have happened to the child if they had not decided to interpret the elf's friendship with the baby in terms of their human understanding. The elf was there to help them work on their farm because they were good people, and he liked them. On the other hand, they decided that the babysitting he was doing to help them was wrong and wanted to repay his kindness with evil. So, they learned their lesson the hard way.

So, they were advised that they would be better off if they would not try to interpret what was in another person's mind. Again, they would do better if they had a second opinion on something crucial like what happened.

The couple were sorry for their baby's death, but they were more sorrowful about what they had done to the elf who had helped them for many months with their work. They felt like they had killed the hen that laid the golden eggs! We can all share the couple's story because we have listened to a friend's advice and hurt other people trying to help us. We can now learn the lesson as the couple in the story did. Some proverbs and wise sayings that can go with a story like this would be:

Nobody hates someone bringing them the news!

If one goes to a funeral with an insulting attitude that person may be sent home with a slap!

When someone else is in pain, because it is not on us, we assume the pain is on a tree.

Sometimes when we think something is going to hurt another person, it ends up hurting us!

Negative thinking destroys a town.

You bought salt to give as a gift, but in return they gave you pepper as a thank you.

Double slaps make one dizzy!

A wound given by a word is harder to cure than that given by the sword.

THE REASON WHY SPIDERS HAVE FLAT HEADS

Once upon a time, there was a great famine in the land where Mr. Spider lived. The famine was so severe that no one could find anything to eat. Mr. Spider decided to go in search of food so that he would not die of hunger, so he set out from his village into the unknown world. He walked and walked for days without seeing anybody. Mr. Spider was beginning to get tired and discouraged when he heard some music from a distance. Mr. Spider picked up his courage and continued walking even though he was exhausted, hungry, and weak from exhaustion.

After what seemed like an eternity to Mr. Spider, he finally drew closer to where the music was coming from. He quickly identified the specific spot and walked to the place, and to his surprise, he saw six men who had barred a portion of a stream and were using a small calabash bow to clear the water out from the barred area to catch the fish inside. (We call that kind of fishing in Ghanaian language, Ahwew.)

The men were singing the following song:
Odomankoma bo adze, Okatakyi boadze obi nhew hensu yi bie!
Gyaa ye ooo woboa ooo gya ye ooo!
Obi nnhwew yensu yi bie
Gyaa ye ooo woboa ooo gya ye ooo!

The literal translation of the music in English: Since Creator created the world, the Almighty created the world; let someone help us drain this water. The response is: Stop it; it never may happen!

The men were using the song's rhythm to try to get the water out of the barred area as fast as they could. Mr. Spider was overly excited when he saw the men and said hello to them with all the energy he could master. They looked up and said hello to him in return. He asked the men if it was all right to join them in fishing. The men responded that it was all right with them, but asked Mr. Spider what he would use to pick up the water. Mr. Spider, in turn asked them where they got theirs, so he could go and find one for himself. To his astonishment, they replied that it was the back of their heads that they had taken off to do the work. Mr. Spider then asked that his should be removed for him to use to do the job as well.

At first, the men hesitated, but then there was nothing they could do to help him except remove the back of his head. Mr. Spider joined the group after the back of his head was cleared for him to work. He sang the song with them as he quickly learned the song's words and rhythm. About late afternoon, the men stopped working, divided the fish they had caught up till then, and gave Mr. Spider his share. They told him not to sing the song on his way home because if he did, the back of his head would fall off again.

He promised he would not sing the song, but as soon as he parted company with them, he started humming the tune and suddenly began to sing because he liked the rhythm and the words. As soon as he sang the song, the back of his head fell off. He quickly picked it up and started running after the men screaming, "Please, please, help me." One of the men heard his screams and told the rest that Mr. Spider was screaming after them for help and that he thought he may have sung the song. The men started to walk back to meet Mr. Spider, who was carrying the back of his head in his hands and screaming his head off. The men put it back on and strictly warned him not to sing the song because if he did, he might not find them again to put it back on for him.

Mr. Spider thanked them and departed toward his village with his share of the fish. When he reached the village, and his friends saw him with a big basket full of fish, they wanted to know where he got them. He was so excited to tell them that he had forgotten the warning not to sing the song, and he began to demonstrate to them how he came by the fish and began to sing.

As soon as he began singing, the back of his head fell off, and he started screaming and running towards the river searching for the six men, but he never found them. After searching for days and days without success, Mr. Spider finally gave up and went home. That is why spiders have flat heads today!

There are many lessons to be learned from Mr. Spider's story so that we do not repeat what he did by not listening to the advice of the six men who helped him find food for his family but told him not to sing the song.

Some proverbs and wise sayings to go with this story would be:

If you do not pay heed to what you are told, you will have to face what comes out of it!

To obey is better than to sacrifice!

A bad situation sometimes is attached to good ones. (Mr. Spider got the food he needed but ended up with a flat head.)

If the cow is mad, that does not mean the owner too is mad.

If one encounters a situation alone, who would be his or her witness?

If you refuse to listen to advice, you end up in a town where no one listens to anyone!

THE REASON WHY THE DOG CATCHES
THE FLY

Once upon a time, there lived a hunter who had several dogs. He trained his dogs to hunt animals without him, and most of the time, when he was too busy with housework, he would send the dogs into the bush to hunt. They were incredibly happy together because the man cared for them and gave their absolute best services to their master. In a nearby village lived a fly and his family, and occasionally the fly and the dogs would have an opportunity to visit. The dogs did not know that the fly was very jealous of their relationship with their master and so was looking for a chance to destroy the existing harmony between them.

One day, such an opportunity came when the hunter sent the dogs into the bush and visited with his friends in a bar, bragging about his good fortune because of his dogs. The fly happened to pass by the bar and heard what the hunter was saying, and it made him mad that the hunter was sitting in a bar drinking while the dogs were working extremely hard in the bush for him. The hunter, however, had prepared the dogs' food and left it in their usual place to eat when they returned from hunting.

On the other hand, the fly followed them and went into the bush searching for the dogs. When he found them sweating and busy with their game, he asked them why they were killing themselves for a man who cared nothing about them. The dogs were incredibly angry with the fly for saying such things, and they told him that their master took good care of them, and even now, while they were working, their food was being cooked at home for them.

The fly told them that they were just kidding themselves because he had just passed their master sitting in a bar drinking and bragging to his friends how stupid they were because all he needed to do was to give them the command, and they were running like crazy. The dogs were terribly upset with the fly for lying about their master, so the fly told them to come and see for themselves if he was telling them a lie.

The dogs left their game in the bush and followed the fly into the bar, and sure enough, there was their master a little tipsy, chatting away with his friends. The dogs were so furious that they just started biting him, and by the time his friends realized that it was severe, they had killed him. As soon as that was done, the fly disappeared among the people while everybody was saying how the hunter had just sat there and praised his dogs for their services. The dogs took off and went home, but before they could reach the house, they smelled the odor of their food; and when they reached their feeding place, there were extra bowls filled with meat and food for them. The dogs took off to the fly's house, but he was long gone!

The dogs swore they would never forgive the fly for what he had done and vowed that they would kill him too for deceiving them into killing their master. The dogs were deeply sorry for not going home first to check about their food before following the fly into the bar, but it was too late. Nobody would forgive them and take them into their homes; they wandered around the village aimlessly until they all died. That is why all dogs catch the fly anytime it comes around them.

This story has a lot to be learned about how deception and jealousy can destroy relationships. Even though these are stories about animals, they help us reflect on humans as well; how many times have supposed friends destroyed their friends because they were either jealous or envious of them? Proverbs and wise sayings that will go with a story like this would be:

It is through many friendships that the crab ended up having no head!

Bad company ruins a family!

An aggravator is worse than the devil!

When a bad person lives in a town, the town never prospers!

A town never has peace if there is a gossiper living in it.

Jealousy destroys a town.

When a deceiver lives in a town, the town never prospers!

Hatred has no medicine!

THE KING WHO WANTED AN HEIR

An exceedingly long time ago, a king and queen lived with several daughters; but try as they might, they could not have a son to inherit their throne when they died. This created such a problem for both that they tried many ways to seek help from the local priests and priestesses, but without any success. One day a friend told them about a Malam who was very skillful in such matters, so they decided to travel to the village where this Malam lived to see if he could help them. They set off one fine morning with all kinds of gifts to buy the favor of the Malam, even if he did not have time to attend to their needs right away. When they arrived, they found that the Malam was home and was willing to assist them in whatever way he could with their troubles.

First, the Malam consulted his oracles to see if there was any good news for them. After a while, he turned to face them to give them the hopeful message that would ease their troubles forever, but also the hard prediction that came with the promise. The prediction was that the wife would surely become pregnant again, and this time she would have a son; but when the son reached the age of 14, he would have sex with a woman and would die. The only remedy would be if they could prevent the situation until he passed that age.

The king and queen agreed to protect their son from such an experience until he was above that age, so it happened as they were told. A son was born to them the following year, which brought great jubilation to the town's people because they would now have a king when the present king died. As the boy matured, so did his beauty and wisdom, and everyone loved him. On his 13th birthday, the couple began to worry about the oracle, so they decided to build the boy a house in the forest away from everyone, especially women, until he was 15, when they would bring him back to town. Within a noticeably short time, the house was constructed with beautiful iron bars and an iron gate that no one could enter without being let in, including the parents themselves. The only people visiting him were his parents and the servants who took the boy's food and cleaned his house daily. Even these attendants must ring the doorbell on the iron gate to be let in.

The boy was very content and happy with his new environment and was grateful that his parents cared that much about him. One day, something strange happened because the girls in the village decided to go to the forest in search of firewood. When one girl got lost in the forest, she went deeper into the forest instead of going toward the village until she was totally lost. As evening approached, she saw the light in the distance and thought she had finally reached home. To her astonishment, she saw an unusual, beautiful house with iron bars that no one could get inside. She also noticed the doorbell, so in her fear, she rang so loud that the boy woke from his nap to look out the window, wondering who it might be since the servants had just returned home from his house. As he looked out, his gaze fell upon an exceptionally beautiful girl half scared to death outside his gate, so he came down to find out what was the matter with her. As he got closer, his heart started beating faster without any cause. He reached the gate and opened it for her to step in, and her heart also started beating faster without any reason. They looked at each other and fell in love right away. The boy kindly invited the young woman into the house to have something to eat and to rest since she had been lost for a whole day and later to point the way for her to go home without any trouble.

After they both walked into the house, the young man kindly offered his guest bathing water. She took a quick bath and looked so beautiful that the young man could not resist anymore and decided to make his love plain to her; he invited her to stay the night, telling her that he would let his servant take her home in the morning. The girl agreed to stay and not go home since it was so dark outside and because she knew that her parents would not come looking for her until tomorrow.

They went to bed together and had sex in the night when to the young woman's surprise, the young man died right afterward! She was so terrified that she ran home in the early morning hours since he had shown the right direction to her during their conversation. After she went home, she told no one what had happened to her since no one knew there was such a house in the forest.

Some hours later, there were a lot of hushed conversations among the inhabitants of the area because the servants went to visit as usual, and the gate was open, and the young prince was dead. The king and queen immediately knew what had happened and started an investigation among the young women in the town, but no one knew about the house in the forest, and no one had been there. The king and queen went to the forest, brought the boy's body home, and sent for the Malam to come and see if there was anything he could do to help. He replied that he would follow the messengers immediately as soon as he could get away. They waited and waited, but the Malam was nowhere to be seen. So they laid the prince in state for burial, and the people started weeping and wailing for the young prince who never had the opportunity to inherit the throne after all. Two days passed, and still, the Malam was nowhere to be seen, but on the third day, when they were ready to put the prince in the coffin for burial, there were shouts everywhere that the Malam had arrived. The message reached the parents before the Malam himself reached the palace.

When he arrived at the palace, he noticed that the body was still on the bed with the coffin opened and ready for the prince's body to be placed in it for burial. The king and queen spoke at the same time. "How good to see you, Paa Malam, and is there something you can do to help?" The Malam answered in the affirmative. "Yes, there is something I can do to help if you can cooperate with me." They both said yes, they would do anything in their power to help.

The Malam asked for a bonfire to be made, and immediately all the women in the town started bringing firewood from their houses; within a truly short time, there was a massive fire burning. The Malam then said to the king, "You are his father. Jump into the fire; your son will wake up as you burn." The king asked, "What about my other children? Yes, I needed an heir, but I am not ready to kill myself for just one dead son." The man turned to the queen and said, "Well, you are the mother. Would you jump into the fire for your only son?" The queen answered, "If his father, who wanted a boy so much, was not willing to jump into the fire for his son, what made you think I am going to leave my daughters and die for just one son?" So the Malam said to them, "If you did not need a son that much, why were you so worried about his death?"

At that moment, the girl who had sex with the young man and unknowingly caused his death came forward. She asked the Malam if it would be possible for anyone who loved the prince to jump into the fire and burn for him so that he would wake up, to which the Malam said yes. The girl asked the Malam to wait for just a few minutes, and she would be back. The girl went home and took her picture and the cloth she wore that night she met the prince. She returned and handed these things to the Malam with the following remark. "Give this to the boy when he awakes, and tell him that this was the woman who jumped into the fire and burned herself so he could come back to life." Everyone thought the girl was out of her mind, including her parents, who could not deter her from what she wanted to do. She knelt and prayed, and after that, she went exceptionally far away from the fire and ran full speed and leapt into the flames; but as soon as she jumped, the fire died out, and no harm came to her.

Suddenly, there were loud shouts and screams from the palace hall where the boy's body had been laid in state. "He is up; he is up, he is up!" The Malam took the young woman by the hand, went into the palace, and said to the boy, "This is the one who killed you, and she is also the one who loved you enough to sacrifice her life for you. From now on, the two of you have become one flesh; what your mother or father could not do for you, your wife would do for you." That is why when a man marries; the woman becomes his sole life. Again, that is the reason for the deep love between a wife and a husband that has been going on for generations.

The parents thanked the young woman for her bravery while the prince asked for her hand in marriage. They lived to be incredibly old and had many children and grandchildren. When they finally succeeded on the throne, they became the couple everyone wanted to imitate because they were like brothers and sisters to each other.

There are lots of lessons from this story that we all can learn. Proverbs that would be used with this story would be:

One cannot hide from one's own destiny!

The water that loves you is the one that flows into your drinking container!

When a woman loves you, she does not care if you wear tattered clothes!

Love covers a multitude of sins!

God works in mysterious ways!

What God has ordained cannot be thwarted.

HOW MONKEYS SPREAD
THROUGHOUT THE WORLD

Once upon a time, a princess was so beautiful that she refused to marry any man until she found one who was as handsome as she was beautiful. Many extraordinarily handsome men came and tried to win her love but failed because there was always something wrong here or there as far as she was concerned. The news about this beautiful, impossible princess traveled far and wide; the more the news spread, the more suitors came from far and wide to try to win her love. After she had rejected far more princes than was necessary, her parents told her that since she had been through so many suitors, they would not accept any more. However, the day she finally found the man she loved, she should come to them and indicate her decision in whatever way she wanted, so she agreed.

As man after man was sent away, many of the townspeople became very aggravated and frustrated with the princess's strict standards for a suitor. Finally, a monkey turned himself into the most handsome man you have ever seen or could ever imagine and proceeded to the town where the princess lived. As soon as he entered the town, many heads were turned toward the incredibly handsome stranger as almost everyone who saw him fell in love with him at once. As usual, the suitor went straight to the house of the most beautiful princess to try his luck. He was received by her maids and shown to the reception room.

As soon as his shadow fell upon the princess, she raised her eyes to see who had come in this time to try to win her love and her eyes met the man's at the same time, and that was it. She jumped out of her chair and went straight to her mother in the kitchen, where she was cooking banku (cornmeal). The princess immediately took the banku cooking stick and hit her mother on the head with it. Her mother's friends who were present accused the princess of disrespect, but her mother defended her, saying, "Leave her alone because this is a sign that she has finally found a suitor." Again, she ran out to where her father was drinking with his friends and acted the same; she took the calabash from her father's hand and smashed it on his head. The people around him also accused the princess of disrespect, but her father defended her action and said, "Leave her alone. She has finally found a suitor with whom she is in love and is ready to marry him."

Everyone was incredibly happy when they heard the news that the perfect man for the princess had finally arrived. The proposal was received with great joy, and the princess was more radiant than she had ever been. The time was set for the marriage, and you can imagine what the ceremony was like! It was something you wished you had seen or been a part of because there has never been anything like it again. The festivities went on for months and when it was all over, the husband had to leave with his wife. So they were provided with a hundred strong male and female servants to go with them since they had to travel to a distant country partly on foot. The day came for the couple's departure, and everyone in town came to wish them happiness and to say goodbye to the most extraordinarily beautiful couple you will ever come across. They left, rode for a while, and eventually came to the place where they had to make the journey on foot. So the husband told the servants to unload the car and carry the loads on their heads because they had to take the bush path. The servants unloaded the car and shared the load so that everything was carried. The procession began descending into the thick forest where you would think no human being would survive, but they had no choice since they were following the groom's orders.

They went half a day's journey on foot when suddenly the man stopped and said to the company, "This is my home." Everyone was horrified when they turned and could not see the road they just came from again. They did not realize that the road was closing behind them as they went. There was no way to return except to push through the weeds if one was determined to return. The princess and company were still thinking about what to do when suddenly the man started to sing:

Tee tee kalamba
Tee tee kalamba
Koforidua kalamba
Koforidua kalamba
Tee..............! Kyere me dan.

Immediately, the man turned into a huge monkey and started jumping from tree to tree, as happy as he could be. The princess exclaimed in a loud voice, "What is this? Some kind of magic? Or spell that is cast when you say the words, "kyere me dan." As soon as the words "kyere me dan" came out of her mouth, she too turned into a monkey and leapt after her husband. Everyone was trying to figure out why those words, once spoken, had entrapped the couple in some magical world—or just what had happened to them. But they were not wise enough to realize that the words "kyere me dan" were affecting them all. So they also were turned into monkeys, except for one girl who never spoke.

The only human being left was the girl who never spoke, so she decided to go back home and tell everything she had seen to her family. She traveled all day and rested on the tops of trees for protection during the night until she found a farm and followed the path back to her town. She never spoke to anybody for fear that something might happen to her before she got home. When she arrived, everybody was surprised to see her so thin; they were also disturbed to learn that she had not spoken to anyone who greeted her on the way. People knew there must be something terribly wrong with her, but at the same time, they respected her silence. She went to the king's house and conveyed to him that she would not speak until he assembled the whole town so they could hear what she had witnessed. The king instantly sent people to beat the gon-gon to summon everyone to the community center for an emergency meeting. Within half an hour, the community center was packed full, with the girl sitting by the king's side.

Before the girl began her story, she asked to be tied to a pole with strong ropes. Everyone thought it was odd that she wanted to be tied tightly to a pole, but if that was what it took to hear what she had to say, so be it. She narrated to the king and the community how their pleasant journey by car ended suddenly, forcing them to walk and carry their possessions on their heads for the rest of the trip.

She also told them how the groom took them through a very thick forest and then told them that was his home in the middle of nowhere. They had no way of knowing that the handsome man was not a human being who lived in a house, but a monkey who made his home in the trees.

She also told the king how they had suddenly turned around to look behind them and could not see the road they had just traveled on; everything was just a thick forest. They were in the middle of that shock when the groom suddenly burst into song. Then the girl stopped short and asked again to be made securely tight before she would sing the song the man sang. Some of the people thought the girl was creating a monster out of an ordinary ant, but the king, however, made sure her request to be tied securely to the pole was accomplished. After that, she started to sing:

Tee tee tee kalamba
Tee tee tee kalamba
Koforidua kalamba
Koforidau kalamba
Tee.............! Kyere me dan!

As soon as she sang the words "Kyere me dan," the ropes around her burst into pieces like bread, and she turned into a monkey and started jumping up and down before their eyes. Everyone was so surprised that they started saying, What kind of magic is this that happens when you say, "Kyere me dan?" And they, too turned into monkeys! Before too long, everyone in the town had turned into a monkey, jumping up and down and leaping through the trees. So, the once flourishing town full of people soon turned into a town filled with monkeys. Because no one was left to sing the song to affect other towns and cities, the magic ended there.

There used to be only one monkey in the world, and if it had not been for the beautiful, impossible princess who would not marry any man but the one who matched her in beauty, this would not have happened. This story explains a great deal, including why monkeys have increased in population and why all monkeys act like human beings. Furthermore, it helps us understand why many people do not want to marry someone they did not know before, because one never knows whom one might marry!

Proverbs that would go with such a story would be:

If you put your hand on thirty corpses, one may end up taking you to the grave!

One who asks for directions never gets lost.

If you are the only person who can speak of an event, who would be your witness?

When a huge problem is coming, there is no flag to indicate it!

The words, Had I known, are always heard last or too late.

If you are going to marry, ask questions!

The goat thought it was destroying its owner's house by rubbing its body on it. However, by the time the goat was done, its own skin had been peeled off.

THE REASON WHY GREED AND
DISRESPECT LEAD TO DEATH

Once upon a time, there was a man who had two wives: the senior wife's name was Yeboaba, and the younger's name was Sunkwa. They both were blessed with children, but the senior wife's children were very mean and disrespectful. On the other hand, there was one daughter of the junior wife who was the opposite of her nasty half-sisters and brothers. Everybody in the town loved the children of the junior wife, especially her daughter, which made her rival Yeboaba hate her all the more. Yeboaba was always looking for an opportunity to quarrel with her rival Sunkwa!

One day an opportunity came for Yeboaba to take vengeance on her rival's children, especially her daughter. Sunkwa asked Yeboaba to keep her children while she went to the farm to work with their husband and bring home some foodstuffs. Yeboaba agreed to take care of her rival's children while Sunkwa went to work on the farm for the day, but as soon as the couple left for farm, she started plotting what she could do to hurt her stepdaughter. Madam Yeboaba cooked mashed yams and made a nice yam porridge and shared it among all the children, but before she gave the porridge to her stepdaughter, she put her trinket into the porridge. Innocently, as she was eating, the stepdaughter cracked her teeth on something hard, so she took it out and realized that it was a trinket.

She showed it to her stepmother, who screamed at her for breaking her trinket. The girl explained to her that she did not know how it got into her food, but Madam Yeboaba started calling her names anyway. She then ordered her stepdaughter to go to a well-known cruel god of a distant town to get another trinket for her, without waiting for her mother to come back home from the farm. The god's name was "bosom nnkegyaa," meaning a god who will not spare you when he gets you. The awful part of this journey into this god's domain was that one must pass all kinds of tests by meeting fierce animals before one reaches the presence of this god if one ever gets there at all.

The girl wanted to wait for her parents, especially her mother, but her stepmother would not let her. So she set out on her journey, knowing that she might never see her parents again. Her brothers cried with her and gave her courage that she may return safely, by the grace of God, since she did not know who put the trinket in her food. The girl was also worried that her going away on this dangerous errand might cause a fight between her parents, and she felt responsible for that too. You can imagine her fear and frustration. She started praying to God for protection as she set off into the unknown. As she went a little further along the road, she met a cat who asked her where she was going on that road, knowing that it was a dangerous road. The young girl started singing:

Girl: Adende my mother went to the farm.

Response: Adende

Girl: Whom did she leave me with?

Response: Adende

Girl: She left me with her rival

Response: Adende

Girl: Rival Madam Yeboaba

Response: Adende

Girl: Mashed her yam and made yam porridge

Response: Adende

Girl: She gave me some to eat.

Response: Adende

Girl: There was a trinket in mine.

Response: Adende

Girl: I have cracked the trinket by mistake.

Response: Adende

Girl: Then she cries, *Hii, hii, hii!!!!*

Response: Adende!

The cat listened with an incredibly sad heart. After the song ended, she said to her, Continue your journey, for you have a very pitiful case. So, the girl took off again and walked for a while before she was confronted with the same question by a huge dog, who said, Where are you going on this road? The girl sang her song again, narrating her sad story to the dog the same way she had done for the cat. After the song was over the dog said, Go your way for you have a sad story. She took off again and went for miles without meeting any person or animal. Suddenly, out of nowhere came a bear and scared her half to death! The bear asked her the same question: Where are you going on this road? The girl was shaking with fear when she started singing, but the bear sat and listened to her song and after the song was over, the bear said, Yours is a very sorrowful case; go your way.

In the meantime, the parents had returned home from their farm, and the stepmother had lied to them that their daughter had gone into her room and stolen her trinket. Furthermore, according to the stepmother, the girl intentionally chewed on the charm and broke it to pieces. Because she scolded the girl and told her that she would report her to her parents, the girl decided to go on her own to bosom nnkegyaa's place for a replacement. The stepmother said she tried to stop her, but the girl would not listen to her pleas. Meanwhile, her brothers told the parents the truth—that Madam Yeboaba made the girl set out on the dangerous journey to find the cruel god. Yet it was hard to understand what had happened because the girl was not there to speak for herself. Even though the parents did not believe Madam Yeboaba's story, everybody knew the result for the girl. As days turned into weeks and weeks turned into months, everyone was sure that the girl had been killed. So they had her funeral, and the mother, and the rest of the town mourned for her for a long time.

In reality, the girl was alive and well and getting closer and closer to bosom nnkegyaa's place. After having several encounters with other animals, she finally reached the most dangerous part of her journey. She was confronted by a large lion that would have killed her on the spot if the god himself had not intervened on her behalf. He said, Leave her alone because she would not have made it here if she did not have a tangible reason to be here. She must be carrying sad news, or she must be on a sad mission.

Bosom nnkegyaa asked the girl to tell him her reason for coming into his presence. The girl sang her song to him, and he asked her to come closer to him and sing her song once more, which she did. After that, bosom nnkegyaa invited the girl to rest for a few days, for the journey had been too much for her and her spirits were low. Once she had rested a little, he would tell her what to do.

Several days later, she was told to go behind the house where she was staying, and there she would find a lime tree full of leaves; she should chew as many as she could and return to him. The girl went and did as she was told. She chewed until she could not chew anymore and came back to report that she had eaten enough. Bosom nnkegyaa asked her to go and chew a little more; so she did until she looked as though she was pregnant with leaves. She was then asked to drink water, which she did. After that, bosom nnkegyaa told her to return home to her parents; she should not go straight home, but instead must go to the town dump. There she will find a familiar girl from the town who had just come to throw away her garbage and was returning home. She should then ask the girl to carry a message to Sunkwa, telling her that the missing girl was on her way home, and that she should cook a yam porridge and put in a large, dried fish (stinking fish).

You can imagine how her mother received the news! Sunkwa quickly prepared the food, and as soon as the food was ready, the girl arrived. For the first time in a long time, the mother was able to eat a good meal too. The girl's belly was so big that everyone thought she was pregnant. As she ate, she swallowed a fish bone that got caught in her throat and started throwing up. Guess what? She was throwing up gold nuggets! Soon the house was filled with gold, and she was still throwing up. So they moved her to another house, and that one too was filled up. Then they moved her to another house, and that one too was filled up. Gold was everywhere! By the time she stopped, her stomach was as thin as it was before she ate so many lime leaves. She told her parents what had happened to her and how she was afraid she would never see them again, but God protected her.

In the end, they filled six baskets full of gold for her stepmother to repay her for the one trinket that was broken. But she would not accept them because she said it wasn't enough, since it was her fault that the girl had brought home all that gold. Madam Yeboaba decided that she had children too, and one of her own must go and get more gold from bosom nnkegyaa's place. So she told one of her daughters to go and break Sunkwa's golden pot and then go and get some gold from bosom nnkegyaa. But her daughter replied that her stepsister did not do that. Instead, her mother made up a lie as part of a plot that would end with the death of the innocent girl. Well, Madam Yeboaba was furious with her daughter, and told her that if her half-sister had refused to obey, her family would not have been rich. In the end, the daughter had no choice but to obey her mother. So she destroyed her stepmother's beautiful golden pot. Even though Sunkwa did not say a word to her about the broken pot, Madam Yeboaba still insisted that her daughter must make the dangerous journey to bosom nnkegyaa's place to collect some gold; so, she set out as nasty as she can be.

Just as she entered the road, she met the cat who asked her where she was going. Oh my, she was wild! She started insulting the cat as though it was the cat's fault that she was taking this journey. The cat said to her, I am just too little for you, but go ahead, and you will meet your match, and disappeared into the bush. It was not long before she met the dog, and the dog asked her the same question, Where are you going? The girl was very offended and started screaming at the dog as she had done to the cat. She said, Get away from me with your stupid questions. Is it not my mother who told me to go and break my stepmother's golden pot and to go to bosom nnkegyaa's place and bring some gold back for her? The dog also said to the girl, I am only a kid. Go ahead, and you will meet your match!

Her next meeting was with a bear. As soon as the bear saw her, it moved into the road and asked her the same question: Where are you going on this road? The girl started shouting at the bear, but the bear gave her one blow and killed her instantly. The bear put her body in a nice box and brought it to the place where the first girl had appeared when she came home and deposited it there.

In the meantime, her mother had been spying on the place every day to see if her daughter would appear suddenly, then she would be the one to see her first. One day as she visited the site, she saw a lovely box and she quickly ran home to prepare the special yaw porridge with fish. She thought to herself that her daughter was so beautiful and important that she did not have to walk home as did her rival's daughter. After she finished cooking the food, she asked her neighbors to bring the box home for her. When the box had been brought in, they called out her name to come and eat because the food was ready, and no answer came. They tried again and again, and nothing happened, so they decided to open the box, and as they did, they were greeted by a foul smell and flies. Suddenly, the woman realized that her daughter had been killed, and she started screaming.

But whose fault was it? If she had not been so mean and greedy, her daughter would not have been killed this way. So, it became a lesson for the whole village that if you want your children to succeed, you should treat other children with love and care too! The proverbs that go with such a story would be:

If you do not allow your friend to get nine, you will not get ten.

Rivalry is like cow dung; when the top is dried then the bottom is still very wet.

If one collects poisonous medicine to kill someone, eventually some will touch your lips.

Bad character will always send a person away.

Greed never leads one to a good place.

THE REASON WHY MEN'S CHESTS GROW HAIRS

An exceedingly long time ago, both men and women had no hairs on their chest until the following incident happened: Once there was a man who had two wives. One wife had children, and the other had none. The one with children would tease the one with no children until one day, she could stand it no longer. She decided to search for someone who would help her get a child of her own. In her search she met a medicine man who promised he could help her get pregnant if she would follow all the restrictions and instructions that he would give her. Furthermore, she must be able to protect the child from exposure to certain kinds of foods. One of those foods is ewuruku (a kind of yam we have in Ghana), because he would make the medicine from that kind of yam. The medicine man told her that the very day that the child touched that yam, they will die. The woman promised to protect herself as well as the child from those dangers if she can give birth.

The medicine man gave her the medicine and sure enough she became pregnant. When the time came for her baby, she had a baby girl on a Monday, so she was named Adwoa Kuma, because the man's senior wife also had a girl named Adwoa, and so Adwoa Kuma means Adwoa Junior. As the child grew, so did her beauty. Adwoa Kuma became the talk of the town for her beauty as well as for her good manners; everyone loved her because she was such a good-natured person. This made the other wife terribly angry and jealous since her rival's child was receiving most of the attention from the people. In her anger and jealousy, she plotted to get rid of the girl if she ever got the opportunity by giving her what she could not eat or touch.

One day, the opportunity presented itself when the girl's mother innocently asked her rival to take care of her daughter while she ran to collect some food from her farm. Adwoa Kuma was about eight years old at the time, and her mother thought she could defend herself from what she could not eat well. As soon as Adwoa's mother left for the farm, her rival quickly took ewuruku, peeled it, and asked Adwoa Kuma to carry the garbage to the dumping area. The girl told her stepmother that she was not supposed to touch that yam or even look at it. Her stepmother became furious with her and commanded her to carry the garbage to the dumping area on the outskirts of the village.

The girl had no choice but to obey her stepmother, so she carried the ewuruku peels and set out toward the dumping ground. She wept as she went. The village was noticeably quiet at that hour of the day because most of the people had already gone to the farm. However, there was a young girl who was sitting outside the village gate because she had yaws, who saw Adwoa Kuma as she carried the garbage out from her stepmother's house while she wept on her way to the dumping ground. She also saw Adwoa Kuma on her way back to the village, and how the earth opened up and swallowed her.

In the meantime, Adwoa Kuma's mother returned from her farm and asked her rival about Adwoa Kuma's whereabouts. Her rival told her that Adwoa Kuma was just playing outside a second ago with the other children, but she did not know where she had disappeared. She even helped her rival by calling out Adwoa Kuma's name. The mother became alarmed when she did not respond to her calls; neither could she find the girl playing anywhere near the neighborhood. The two women searched for her everywhere, and all kinds of assumptions were formulated by the villagers, who were very sympathetic to the worried mother.

When the young girl at the gate heard the lies told by Adwoa Kuma's stepmother and the stories formulated by the villagers, she told the mother the truth about what she saw a while ago.

She explained to the mother how she saw Adwoa Kuma coming from her stepmother's house, carrying garbage, and weeping as she walked to the dumping ground. She also told her how on Adwoa Kuma's way back, she had seen the earth open up and swallow her. The stepmother swore that she knew nothing about what the girl was saying. The people at first did not believe the young girl's story either, since they could not see any disturbance in the ground where the girl pointed as the place where Adwoa Kuma had disappeared.

The mother, in her anguish, set out to go to the village where the medicine man lived. The man was not surprised to see her coming, since he already knew something was wrong. Adwoa's mother fell at the medicine man's feet and told him all of what had happened that morning. However, before the mother's arrival, the medicine man knew about the tragedy and was waiting for her to appear at his doorstep. The medicine man immediately set out with her and came to her village to find out whether the young girl's story was true since the stepmother had denied any knowledge about what the young girl said.

The medicine man collected some herbs, took his medicine wand, and came with Adwoa's mother directly to the spot where the young girl had pointed out as the place where Adwoa had disappeared. He put the herbs he brought there, said some prayers, and hit the medicine with his medicine wand. (The wand was a "horsetail," which he used for such significant performances.) Suddenly, the earth opened, and sure enough, there deep down in the world was Adwoa's hair. The medicine man started to sing the following song:

To translate the song in English word for word is somewhat difficult.

The man called out: Adwoa Kuma. (Repeat)

Response: Softly, softly!

The day had broken for children to fetch water.

Response: Softly, softly!

Again, the day had broken for children to fetch firewood.

Response: Softly, softly!

But in her case, the earth and the dust have conspired together to take her away.

Response: Softly, softly!

As soon as the first song was finished, Adwoa Kuma pushed up a little. The man continued to sing, and Adwoa continued to push upwards until one child screamed her name out when she saw

Adwoa Kuma coming out of the ground. The medicine man asked all the children to be called into the village, to call Adwoa Kuma out, or she would not come when her name was shouted out. All the children were sent out from the place into the village, and their parents asked to watch over them so that they did not sneak in until Adwoa was entirely out.

The man had to start all over again, and Adwoa Kuma came up with each song that was sung until her toes were almost out. But before the man could sing the last piece to get her out, another child sneaked out and screamed her name. By that time, however, the hole had closed enough behind her that it was too late for Adwoa Kuma to go back into the hole. So instead, she jumped into the medicine man's bosom and immediately turned into hair. That was the reason why men began to grow hairs over their chests. So, when you see somebody with a chest full of hair, remember the beautiful eight-year-old girl named Adwoa Kuma, whose wicked stepmother's jealousy made her turn into strands.

Proverbs to go with a story like this would be:

When you do evil, it follows you, and when you do good, it too follows you!

Jealousy has no medication!

When one plants a hypocritical corn, it germinates on one's heel!

One tells lies where nobody else will ever visit there.

A mother knows what her children will eat.

Your future becomes shaky when your mother dies.

Your clan ends with the death of your mother.

An orphan's life is sympathetic.

THE REASON WHY THE LARGE BLACK
ANT SMELLS LIKE A SKUNK

Once upon a time, God had a messenger who was a hunchback, and part of his work was to help people with his hunchback since it was a magic hunchback. He often helped farmers when he was passing through and found they were having difficulty weeding their plots. He would just ask them to cut a pair of drumming sticks and drum on his hunch gently, and they would see what would happen. At first, people did not want to do it because they were afraid to hurt him, but he continued to insist upon it, and one man took courage to try it. When the man began to drum upon the hunch, it started making a kind of music:

Kunto, kunto.
Response: Wasewa, wasewa!

Kunto kunto.

Wasewa, wasewa!

Within a few minutes, the hunchback had cleared three to four acres of land, to everyone's surprise. They said thank you, and in a second, he was gone, feeling incredibly happy that he had been able to help others with their work. The news spread quickly among the farmers, and soon everybody was trying to find the hunchback to help them with their farm work. The hunchback helped many farmers, so that year, people had an abundant harvest.

The following year, Mr. Spider thought of making a second farm for his family, so he invited God's messenger, the hunchback, to come and help him clear his land. The hunchback agreed on a day that he would go and assist him on his farm. Mr. Spider thought to himself that morning that if tiny drumsticks could produce such a result, then what would larger drumsticks do? Mr. Spider went and cut large drumsticks and hid them ahead of time in the place where they would be weeding that day. When the hunchback arrived, Mr. Spider went and cut the usual tiny drumsticks and started drumming on his hunch. As soon as the weeding started— Kunto, kunto, wasewa, wasewa; kunto, kunto, wasewa, wasewa—Mr. Spider took the larger ones from behind him and started drumming so hard that the hunchback fell to the ground and died.

Now Mr. Spider was scared and tried to revive him, but he was already dead. So, Mr. Spider carried his body to the presence of God and lied that he was just working with him on his farm when the hunchback got sick and died. God said to Mr. Spider that he was the one who killed him. So he could keep the body wherever he wanted, but he should not bury the hunchback on any of the lands he created. Mr. Spider did not know what to do with the body because God would not let him plant the hunchback in the soil.

Mr. Spider was very tired of carrying the hunchback's body, so he left God's presence and started plotting who was going to be his victim to carry the body of God's messenger. As he was going back, he met a black ant, which we call "Adam" in Ghana, who was also traveling on the same road, going the other way. Mr. Spider quickly asked the ant to help him by carrying the body of God's messenger, who had just died from some illness, and had to be returned to God's presence. Since the body of a divine messenger could not be put on the ground, he begged the ant to take the corpse for just five minutes while he went to the toilet.

Mr. Spider did not explain to the ant that God was angry with him for intentionally killing the hunchback, who was God's kind messenger. So, the ant gladly took the corpse from the Spider so he could go to the toilet. When Mr. Spider was relieved of his burden, he quickly told the ant that it takes him longer than an average person to go to the toilet. But for him not to worry, he would tie a rope around his waist and the ant's waist. He explained that when the ant pulled the rope, and the rope was tight, then he was still on the toilet. So, Mr. Spider stepped aside into the bush and waited for a while; when the ant pulled the rope, he responded, I am still here. A little later, the ant called again, and Mr. Spider said, I had not finished yet. As soon as he responded for the second time, Mr. Spider untied his end of the rope, tied it to a tree, and went home, leaving the dead body with the ant.

The ant called and called, but there was no Mr. Spider, and the ant could not bury God's messenger in the ground because God had decreed it so. The ant carried the hunchback looking for Mr. Spider, who had disappeared into thin air, until the body rotted upon him. That is why the ant called Adam smells like a skunk. The proverbs or wise sayings that would be good for such a story would be:

It is painful when someone deceives you!

You bought salt to give as a gift, but you got hot pepper as a thank you!

One cannot hide the evil they have done!

Greed destroys harmony!

Selfishness destroys many good things.

THE CHILDREN WHO RANG THE
CHURCH BELL

Several centuries ago, there was a beautiful city, and, in that city, there was a very unbelievable church building with a magic bell that when it rang produced music. The music was so calming and charming that people flocked into the town just to hear the bell's music. The fame of the church and its magnificent bell spread far and wide throughout many countries. On the outskirts of this great city were many small villages where farmers lived. Most of the farmers were too poor to visit the city to see the bell. But sometimes they would hear the bell ring and its soothing music made them very happy.

Those parents who had been able to visit the church told stories to their children about the wonderful church bell and how its music had charms that calmed people and had drawn many people from other places to come and visit the city. The children listened to the stories in awe and hoped someday they, too, would be able to go and visit the town to see this incredible church bell and hear its magical music for themselves.

Among the farmers was an impoverished family; they were very kind and religious even though they did not have much, and they taught their children to be kind and not treat other people unkindly. Their two boys were taught how to treat all people with respect and kindness, especially the elderly, who should be treated with extra gentleness.

So, the two boys grew up with much love, respect, and kindness for everyone, especially the elders within their community. They loved to listen to the story about the church bell over and over again until they could hear the bell ringing in their dreams.

Suddenly, the bell stopped ringing one day. And no matter what anyone did, the bell would not ring; the sadness and disappointment of people far and near could be felt. So, the priest came up with the idea that during every Christmas season, people would bring a gift to the church, place their offering individually, and see whose gift would please God enough to let the bell ring again. Everyone accepted that, and it also comforted them, knowing they would be doing something to help the bell ring again.

The first Christmas came and went, and nothing happened. So the news spread far and wide, and more people went for the second Christmas, and nothing happened. By this time, the poor farmers had been telling their children about what was required for the bell to ring again. The boys asked their parents if they could go to the Christmas service to see whose gift would ring the bell, and the parents agreed. So they began saving the nickels they earned by working hard for other farmers to take to church on Christmas Day during the service to put in the collection plate. They knew their money would not do much, but they would still be there to see whose gift would please God and ring the bell.

That winter, the snow was worse than usual, but the two boys would not let that stop them from going to church in the city. So, they got their sleds out, even though the snow was coming down steadily, and got themselves ready to go to church. On their way there, they came upon an elderly man who had fallen in the snow and would have died if they had not arrived at the time they did. They stopped to help him, but the younger boy was disappointed about being late and missing what they had worked so hard all year to see. So the older boy asked him just to help him get the old man on his sled, and he would take him home while the younger boy went on to church and could tell him what happened at the church if he was delayed and was not able to get there on time. So, they got the almost frozen man on the sled, and the younger boy continued to go to the city while the older boy took the man home, built a fire, and ensured the old man recovered properly before continuing his trip to the town for the church service.

By the time he arrived at the church, all dirty and wet, everyone's gifts had already been placed on the collection plate; the priest was picking it up to bless them when he saw, out of the corner of his eye, a young boy walking shyly toward the altar. The priest stopped and lowered the plate so the young boy could put his nickel offering into the container. As soon as his nickel dropped into the plate, the bell started ringing *ding-dong, ding-dong*! This scared the young boy so badly that he would have run away if he had not been held back by one of the men.

At this point, everyone was asking who was it that rang the bell and how much he had put into the offering. The priest placed the offering at the altar and brought the young boy up to the front of the church and asked where he had come from and why he was so dirty and wet and almost missed the offering time and the whole service.

By this time, his younger brother had come up to him and was holding his older brother's hand for protection; he told his story about how he was coming with his brother to the service, and they met an elderly man who had fallen in the snow and would have died if they had not come upon him. So, he told his younger brother to go ahead while he took the man home, and since there was no one in the house with him, he made a fire for the elderly man and watched over him until he recovered fully before coming to church. That is why he looks so dirty and almost missed the opportunity to put his nickel into the offering.

The priest thanked him and said the boy's kindness rang the bell again. Because Jesus said, whatever you do for one of the least of my brothers or sisters, you do for me; and so what the boy did for the elderly man was done for Jesus, and Jesus had rewarded him by making the church bell ring again. The priest encouraged everyone to follow the example of the young boy who gave up his own pleasure to save another person's life.

Everyone was very proud of the brothers and gave them lots of gifts for helping not only the old man but also allowing everyone to hear the magic bell and its charming music again. So, the two boys came to the city as the children of poor farmers and went back home rich and famous, using what their parents had taught them to the full!

Proverbs to go with this story would be:

When you do good to others, you are doing it for yourself.

The cup that draws water will always be wet.

If a child is responsive to the needs of others, they enjoy what they like best.

A kind person enjoys favors from others.

When one is open to the welfare of others, one will receive gratitude from others.

The person who shows preferences for others receives the same from others.

One who shows support for another receives the same graces from others.

THE YOUNG WOMAN WHO LEARNED TRUE LOVE THROUGH AN UGLY SCAR ON HER FATHER'S FACE

Many years ago, when the world was not as developed as it is now, there was a village where several farming families lived together as a single community of love, sharing and support for one another. And so the men in the community assisted one another in weeding their farms by taking turns so each one would not have to suffer in doing it alone. Then the women would take turns planting the corn or whatever needed to be planted, and their lives were full of joy and happiness.

What the men would do after their daily work was to gather together to see what needed to be done for whom and at what time. So they planned together, so every one of them was part of the process and that no one was left behind. The women, too, talked together while they cooked their meals; they also shared their needs with each other, especially the mothers among them, if they needed help caring for their children.

The villagers built their own houses with mud and sticks and then made roofs for them with tall grass and banana leaves, all supported by beams made from branches, so the homes would be safe from the rain and sunshine. That was how they lived from generation to generation until one day, something terrible happened to one of the farmers and his family. They had just returned from their daily work and had gathered together as usual and were discussing how the day went and whose turn it was for the following day's work when one man screamed that one house was on fire. So, they all ran to the house and started removing all the things inside, and that man's wife also got the hint that her home was on fire, so, of course, she ran out there also to assist.

In all the confusion, the fire spread quickly over the building, and the couple forgot their youngest daughter, an infant just three months old, was sleeping in the inner room, until the father finally bumped into his wife and asked if she had the baby. She said, No! I thought you had her since you went there first! He decided to go back into the fire with everyone shouting, Don't do it, because, by this time, the baby may have been dead; they knew he was going to risk his life, and if he perished in the fire, he would leave behind four children and a wife. He told them he would never be able to live with himself if he did not try, and even if the baby was dead, at least he could bury her in the ground and not leave her to burn in the fire. He dashed back into the house, and since he lived in that house, he knew how to get into the inner chamber without trouble; when he got there, the baby was still sleeping beneath two of the overhead beams that had fallen halfway down and were hanging above her like a fiery cross. He picked up his child, wrapped her with the cloth she was sleeping on and tried to get out with her. As he reached the outside door, one of the beams that had burned all the way through suddenly broke and fell, hitting him on the right cheek, but he still managed to shield his daughter from harm and carry her to safety. Everyone was so happy that God had protected the child and the brave father, but the wound on his right cheek became an ugly scar on his face for the rest of his life.

All of his five children grew, and he loved them all, but the bond between him and his younger daughter was beyond description; as the girl grew up, she knew how much her father loved her, but no one told her the story of how her father had rescued her from the burning house. She loved her father back but was always wondering what happened to her father's face to give him that ugly scar: was he in a fight or was he into trouble as a young man? She was worried, especially when school children teased her about her father's ugly scar and if her father was a gangster and got shot or hit with something. Children can be cruel and mean when it comes to teasing others, so she carried the pain of this teasing for many years.

She turned out to be a very bright girl, and as life always happens, she finished her elementary studies and went to college, and there too, she was successful and entered a university for her final studies in her field. Nobody knew she was still carrying the pain of her father's facial scar in her heart all the time until one vacation time when she came back home and was having a lovely time with her father, and suddenly she asked, Dad, what happened to your face? That shocked her father, but he said, I will tell you. However, two days went by, and he did not tell her. Again, she asked her father when they were having a good time together and reminded him that he said a couple of days ago that he would tell her, but he did not. The father asked her, Do you want to know what happened to my face? And she said, Yes, I want to know, and the father said, I will tell you. A few days passed, and her father still did not tell her. By now, she was thinking of all kinds of horrible things her father may have done that he did not want her to know about, making her want to know the real story even more desperately!

One afternoon, she and her father were talking, and she asked again, Dad, what happened to your face? You promised you would tell me, but both times you did not. This time her father just said, Get a good chair and sit closer to me and I will tell you since you want to know. She brought the chair, and her father started telling the story to her as I have narrated above, and she sat there listening intently; the father told her everything that happened that day, about their house catching on fire, with all of the villagers assisting them in saving their belongings and how in all the confusion she was left inside the inner room sleeping. Then he got to the part where he finally bumped into her mother and asked about her, and she said she thought *he* had carried her out. The fire by this time had spread everywhere; he said: So everyone advised me not to go back into the burning house looking for you because you may by that time be dead, and I will die too, leaving your mother alone to care for your four senior brothers and sisters. But I decided against their advice and went into the burning house, and you were still sleeping beneath two of the wooden beams that came down and made a cross over you. So I picked you up, and on my way out, one of the beams broke, hit me on the face, and left me with this ugly scar! By the time the father finished telling his daughter the story, she had cried so much that her eyes were all red and swollen. All she could say was, I have always known that you loved me, but I never knew the deepest love you have for me that you were willing to die in the fire for my sake while you had four other children you loved. From that day on, that ugly scar became to her the most beautiful sign of her father's great love for her.

Now, with one single scar, a daughter learned how much her father loved her. Can you see the many scars on Jesus' body and realize how much he loves you to take all the punishment on his head with the crown of thorns? How many scars can you count on his body and all for the love of you? We sometimes do not appreciate what others sacrifice on our behalf until we have the inside story. We do know about Jesus' love for us, but do we truly appreciate it? That is the question we must ask ourselves. Let us learn from this young woman who would not rest until she found the truth about her father's ugly scar on his right cheek and what it all meant!

The proverbs that will go with such a story would be:

If someone does not know who you truly are, they say, that person. But if they do know you, they call you by your name.

It is only a parent who knows how to feed their children.

True love never grows old.

Love conquers fears.

THE REASON WHY THE COCK CROWS: KWEKU EEEEE, SAN BOHWE WO EKYIR OOO!

ENGLISH: KWEKU, RETURN TO WITNESS WHAT IS HAPPENING BEHIND YOUR BACK!

Once upon a time, there was a man named Kweku whose livelihood involved raising chickens. He fed them every day and took good care to give them their medications so that they would not get sick but grow quickly and strong for the market. Every Christmas, Easter, or special holidays he sold his chickens and bought new ones to raise them for another occasion.

Kweku was a good poultry farmer because he knew that his family's income and survival depended upon taking good care of the birds. So, he put a lot of energy into his poultry work. He also kept some of the best fowls for him and his family to feast upon on special celebrations like birthdays, visits from other family members or at Christmas and Easter. So you can imagine why he took such care of the birds.

One day the fowls met and decided that they did not like how Kweku treated them because he sold them only to be killed for soups and stews without any sympathy. Furthermore, he and his family ate the best ones among them, so they had to fight to protect themselves from being eaten as well as being sold. All the fowls agreed upon a plan to fight back from being sold anymore. The plot was to attack Kweku when he came in the morning to feed them in the barn. They agreed that all must attack at once so that Kweku would not be able to fight back or to protect himself from their pecking. So, the fowls' plot was finalized.

The fowls attacked him and killed him early in the morning of the following day when Kweku came to the barn as usual to feed them. When Kweku's family did not see him come back home at the regular time, they did not think much about it at the time. After much time had passed without any message from him, they started getting worried because that was out of Kweku's character. They decided to check on him to see what he was doing that had kept him so long in the barn and why he did not send any message home. To his family's surprise, they found him dead with blood all over his body because of the pecking he had received from all the fowls.

You can imagine how the family felt! The members of Kweku's more prominent family, the community, were beside themselves! They mourned for Kweku for several days, and when the mourning days were over, they performed the burial rituals and buried him. The fowls began to realize the consequences of their action not too long after Kweku's death. They started getting hungry and thirsty since no one else was interested or committed to feeding them and, moreover, carrying on with the poultry work. Because of that, the barns were opened, and the fowls were set free to go and fend for themselves. Consequently, they had to fight each other over the smallest food they could find.

Very quickly the fowls became divided against one another; furthermore, they became easy targets for the foxes, hawks, and birds of prey. Suddenly, they were made aware of the important role Kweku played in their survival. And so the cocks began to call Kweku back with their crows to come and witness what was happening to them behind his back. However, their pleas fell on deaf ears because it was too late since they had already killed Kweku. That is why the cocks still crow for Kweku to come and witness what is happening to them!

This saying is true: "You never know what something is worth until you do not have it any longer!" The fowls learned their bitter lesson by jumping out of the frying pan into the fire! You and I can learn a lesson from the fowl's mistake. Proverbs and wise sayings that go with such stories would be:

When one gathers poison to kill somebody, the same poison will touch their lips!

If you prevent your friend from scoring nine, you, too, will not get the chance to score ten!

To have a little every day to eat is better than having to eat everything in one day!

Evil plots never make one prosper!

Had I known, always comes last.

When you do good, you do for yourself, and when you do bad, you do for yourself.

A bad stomachache does not know I just took medication!

Half a loaf is better than no bread.

HOW FOWLS INHERITED THEIR PRESENT BEAK

An exceedingly long time ago, Mr. Spider and his wife Aso and their children Kweku Tsin, Ntikuma, Efur dotwedotwee (Big Stomach), Nana Nkwankyima, Otsir Kendekendee (Large Head), and Anan Nhwernhwerba (Tiny Legs) lived near where several fowls lived with their families. Some members of the families became such good friends that their children shared games and did the things children in villages normally do when they lived together in harmony. They often went out together to gather fruits when fruits were in season and did lots of other things in common.

One day several children decided to search for kola-nuts because they were in season. The children had no trouble finding what they wanted, because, after a little walk, they found ahead of them, a genuinely nice, loaded kola tree, which was ready to be picked.

They all put their sacks down, and, as usual, Otsi Kendekendee, Large Head, decided to climb the tree to pluck down the kola-nuts for the rest. So, he climbed up the kola-nut tree with such professionalism that the rest of the children admired his skills in climbing. He plucked the kola nuts from the tree so fast that their sacks were filled in no time. However, Otsi Kendekendee would not come down because he wanted to pluck the ones on the very top, which was extremely dangerous since the branches were not strong enough to hold a heavy person like him. The other children tried to persuade him not to go higher because he might fall. However, the more they tried to convince him that it was dangerous, the more he determined to climb higher to the very top. Suddenly, without any warning, the branches he was standing on broke. Because he had such a large head and tumbled down with such force, his head cracked open.

His sister, Tiny Legs, decided to run home to report to her parents. She ran so fast that when she reached the muddy places on the road, her legs broke in the mud because they were too fragile. When the rest came home to report these unfortunate incidents, people could not help but laugh because they always thought Mr. Spider's children looked odd. When the hen heard what had happened, she laughed and laughed and laughed, and when the saliva was running around her mouth, she tried to wipe her mouth with both hands and clasped her mouth in her hand. Because of her unnecessary laughter, her mouth changed from a regular-looking mouth to a beak like the one fowls have now.

Since then, all fowls have inherited the beak-like mouth instead of a regular one. A story like this would be told to entertain but also to help one learn that it is not right to laugh at someone else's expense, especially when it is a tragedy or misfortune. A proverb or wise saying to go with such a story would be:

When you see someone's beard is burning, you fetch water and put it ready by your side.

It is only a fool who would say it happened to my friend, but it will not happen to me!

To obey is better than to sacrifice!

If you refuse to listen to advice, you end up in a stubborn town.

Greed always comes with death.

One must learn to accept one's limitations.

A child that will not let her mother sleep will not sleep either!

THE WOMAN WHO ACCIDENTALLY
KILLED ALL HER CHILDREN

Many centuries ago, there was a woman who lived in a small village with her husband and seven children. The couple were very hard-working, but unfortunately, their six sons were very lazy boys. Just one child, Esi, the only girl, was as hard-working as her parents. No matter what the parents did to the boys, they would not go with them to work on the farm or even go to fetch water for their parents when they were away working on the farm. All they did was recklessly eat the food that the couple and their daughter Esi produced from their sweat.

The boys were a drain on their parents; not only that, but they were also known as the bullies in town because of their ruthless attitudes toward others. The boys' ruthless behavior put the couple on edge and gave them headaches since people kept bringing complaints all the time to them, and they had to go and apologize on their behalf. Furthermore, the boys would always wait until the parents were at the farm, and they would cook all the food in the house for the whole family for the evening and eat it by themselves. They were a burden on their parent's nerves.

Finally, the mother reached her limits and decided upon a plan to kill her sons by putting poison in the cornmeal used to make banku. She knew that as soon as she and her husband and Esi left home to work on the farm that her greedy sons would rush home and use the cornmeal to cook banku for themselves, then eat it all before their parents came home; this time, however, their greed would prove fatal, as this meal would be their last.

The mother told no one what she had done, and the following day she left for the farm with her husband and daughter as usual. That day, the daughter Esi worked amazingly fast at the farm. When she finished her portion of the work, she decided to sneak back home to cook dinner for her parents as a surprise so that they did not have to wait to eat their dinner.

On the other hand, the boys were up to their usual tricks. So they rushed home, thinking they could cook the cornmeal and eat all of the banku themselves before their parents and sister returned. As soon as they put the water on to boil, they sent the youngest brother to go and fetch the cornmeal so that it would be ready for them to cook when the water boiled. They waited and waited, but he never came back, so when the water started to boil, they asked the next youngest one to go and find out what he was doing and if he did not find the cornmeal. He went and saw his brother lying on the floor by the cornmeal and yelled at him, "You are still a kid; look, we are waiting for you, and here you are sleeping." He, too, went and put his hand in the cornmeal, and immediately, the poison affected him, and he died instantly. So, it happened to all six boys; they died one after the other, starting with the youngest and ending with the oldest.

While this was happening, Esi was on her way home to come and cook dinner to surprise her parents. She arrived and found the water boiling for the banku with the fire under it almost died out, and there was no one around. So, she went and changed her farm clothes and came back to cook the banku as usual. When she went inside the cornmeal room, to Esi's surprise, her brothers were all lying there, sleeping on the floor beside the cornmeal. She exclaimed, "Oh, you have worn yourselves out, and now you can't even open your eyes to cook a meal for yourselves?" She went ahead to tend to the work that she came home to perform, but as soon as she stretched out her hand to take some of the cornmeal, she also died instantly.

A bird was sitting on a tree near the house called Apa nhwerom, watching the tragic incident happen. After Esi's death, the bird flew away and went straight to the couple's farm and started narrating what had happened to the woman in a song:

The woman, the woman
Chorus: Your children are finished
The woman, the woman
Chorus: Your children are finished
You grind the corn
Chorus: Your children are finished
You mushed it up
Chorus: Your children are finished
You took the medicine
Chorus: Your children are finished
You put it in the cornmeal
Chorus: Your children are finished
This one touched the cornmeal and died
That one touched the cornmeal and died
Another one touched it and died
Your daughter, Esi, who would have grown to be a great person, also touched the cornmeal and died.

The bird kept following the woman and singing the song as she moved from one area to another until the woman became angry with the bird and threw some gravel at it. The bird flew away and came right back and started the song again, which made the woman uncomfortable, because she knew what she had left in the house, but she did not realize that Esi had left the farm and gone home without informing her. After a while, she felt so distressed that she decided to call Esi so they could go home. She called aloud for Esi several times, but there was no response from Esi anywhere. The woman became extremely nervous and anxious to go home. So she told her husband that Esi had disappeared from the farm, so they needed to go home to check if she had sneaked away from the farm early without telling them. Her husband tried to persuade her that maybe Esi had gone to fetch water, because Esi would have informed them if she went home. However, they soon left and went home early that day.

By the time they arrived at the house, the fire had died out, and the pot was still on the dead fire with a bit of water in the pot. The woman rushed into the cornmeal room and started screaming, bringing her husband to the spot. To his horror and dismay, all seven of his children were spread out in the cornmeal room, dead! The couple's screams and wailing brought people from all corners of the village to see what had happened to them. When people came, they could not believe what their eyes saw, seven beautiful children, all killed in one day because of the ruthlessness of the six boys. The mother learned her difficult lesson the hardest way. A proverb to go with this story would be the following: "If you become too angry with the fly, you end up hitting your wound." That was what the woman did by thinking she could eliminate the problematic and lazy boys and keep her hard-working daughter, but it did not come out that way; she lost all of them, the bad with the good. Other proverbs that will go with such a story would be:

A mother must still love her bad child because she gave birth to them.

If you have a problematic child, continue to feed them because one never knows the future.

When you protect plantain, also preserve the banana because you never know which one will be in season when there is a famine!

One ends up hitting their wound when one gets too irritated with the fly.

A bad apple is permanently attached to a good apple.

When one sheep gets sick, it affects the whole herd.

Experience is the best teacher!

If one has a broken leg, they will learn how to walk.

THE REASON WHY DIFFERENT
ANIMALS CANNOT LIVE TOGETHER

An exceptionally long time ago, different animals used to live together in one village and share things in common as we human beings do. One day the lion, the snake, and the wolf decided to go off together to build a village where they could share things in common and assist each other. First, they built their houses where they would live; then, the lion said it would be a good idea to share with each other what may cause one to become angry with the group so that they could prevent that, if possible, from happening in their relationships.

So, one evening after their daily work, they gathered around the fire to share their dislikes and likes. The snake said that what he dislikes the most is to be stepped upon, so if that happens, he has no choice but to act. The wolf said what he dislikes the most is unnecessary laughter or being laughed at; if that happens, he fights for his rights, even if it leads to death. The lion said he dislikes smelly things the most because that gives him the giggles. With that in mind, the three friends tried to be incredibly careful not to offend one another. So they lived contentedly until one day, the wolf could not find anything to eat all day, no matter how hard he searched for food.

Finally, he came upon some meat in the bush, which he knew may have been leftover meat from the lion's hunt some previous days. The wolf picked it up and brought it home, and the whole place began to smell such a foul odor that the snake began to ask questions about what had happened. Well, the lion came home to this incredible smell from the wolf's kitchen, and he just could not control himself and started laughing. The lion laughed and laughed and laughed as though he could not control his laughter, even though his sides were hurting.

Without any warning, the wolf jumped upon the lion, and the lion was so startled by the sudden jump that he was furious with the wolf for touching him with his smelly paws. They began to fight with each other, and the snake just moved out of their way, realizing how furious they were with each other. They fought for hours and would not stop; they started kicking things over or falling on them, but still, they would not stop. Suddenly, they were in the snake's kitchen area, and the snake was trying to get away from them but was unable to before they stepped upon him.

The snake was so angry with them that he bit them repeatedly to get them off of him, so that by the time they realized what was happening, they both had been poisoned by the snake bites. The three friends were sick for a long period of time. After they recovered, they realized it was not a good idea to live together because they could not prevent such things from happening again since each one has such a temper and is extremely sensitive to their dislikes.

So, they parted company, which is why the lion, the snake, and the wolf do not live together in the same house, but formerly they did. Proverbs or wise sayings that go with such stories would be:

A town that is established with understanding, that is where peace dwells!

Do unto others what you would like them to do unto you.

The palm sticks would not have made a sound if nothing had touched them!

If you aggravate the mute enough, they manage to speak out!

Do not cook stinking fish and put it into my mouth, and then tell me my mouth stinks!

If one cannot pay for the goods, the only decision is for the goods to be returned.

Every pot has its own cover, so how the pot is, so is the cover.

I did not utter the right words is the sister to I did not respond well!

THE REASON WHY GOATS MAKE THE *PII, PII* SOUND AS THOUGH THEY ARE CLEANING SOMETHING FROM THEIR MOUTHS

Once upon a time, the Almighty God made a beautiful farm and planted all kinds of food and vegetables, including a special kind of plantains that bore huge plantains no one had ever seen before. Not far from the farm lived Mr. Spider and his family, so they enjoyed watching Almighty God and his family working on the farm. Almighty God's family only worked during the cooler hours of the morning or late hours of the evening. They planted things, and the farm grew, and the beauty of the plantains was so great that it became the talk of the village; people were wondering where God's family got the root from, so they could buy some.

However, God's family noticed that someone had already harvested the largest plantain ahead of them whenever the plantains were ready for harvesting. This went on for a long period of time until the Almighty God decided to do something about the constantly missing plantains. First, God asked the gon-gon to be beaten throughout their village to see if someone would know who had been stealing the food. Since no one seemed to know, God decided to put a magic syringing tube around the plantain so that the tube would enter the anus of the person who stole the food, so they would find out who the culprit was.

Mr. Spider did not know that God had put this magic tube around the plantain. So he went in as usual in the night to steal when suddenly he found something entering his anus like a syringing tube. He jumped up and landed hard on the big rock, thinking he could crack the tube, but to no avail, even though he tried several times. When God realized that the tube was gone from the plantain the following morning, he quickly put up a considerable sum of money for the town to have a competition in an acrobatic display. This scared Mr. Spider very much. Furthermore, Mr. Spider became aware that the tube was a magic tube in that it disappeared into nowhere during the night and came back during the early morning hours.

However, the announcement of the acrobatic competition gave Mr. Spider an idea. Since he was an excellent acrobatic teacher, he could find somebody to deceive to come and stay in his house for overnight training and pass on the magic syringing tube to him. Mr. Spider started spinning into action immediately since he did not have much time to waste. He thought and plotted whom he might deceive into coming to be the innocent victim of the crime. Mr. Spider's deceptive plot fell on the goat because the goat did not know much about acrobatic display.

Mr. Spider immediately called upon the Goat family and intentionally shared his excitement about the coming competition. When Mr. Goat indicated that he did not know how to perform any acrobatic display or any money to find someone to teach him, Mr. Spider seized the opportunity to offer the Goat family his services free of charge. He would be willing to teach Mr. Goat free of charge since they were friends, and the only requirement would be that Mr. Goat spends some nights at his house since they did not have that much time. Can you imagine the joy of the Goat family?

Mr. Goat went to Mr. Spider's house for some practice and got all excited about the coming competition. So Mr. Spider took advantage of his excitement again and reminded him to come and spend the night at his house so they could work late into the night since the competition was now only four days away. When Mr. Goat came to spend the night, Mr. Spider instructed Mr. Goat to pay attention in the night and not sleep too deep so that when, Mr. Spider, says to him: Move here, move here, he, Mr. Goat, should obey quickly and move, and everything would be fine.

Unfortunately, Mr. Goat was so tired that he slept like a rock the first night, so when the magic tube went out, and Mr. Spider asked Mr. Goat to change places with him, he did not hear a word. The tube again ended up in Mr. Spider's anus where it belonged. You can imagine Mr. Spider's anger the following day with Mr. Goat. It was so bad that Mr. Goat swore he would not sleep like that again and kept his promise that night. When the magic tube went out in the night, Mr. Spider waited until he knew the tube would be coming back in at any moment and asked Mr. Goat to change places with him, which he quickly did. So, the magic syringing tube went into the anus of Mr. Goat instead of Mr. Spider.

You should have seen Mr. Spider the following morning! Mr. Spider was as happy as happy could be and told Mr. Goat that everything was fine and that he could go home, for he was ready for the competition. Mr. Goat had completed the required skills for the acrobatic display so that he would see him the following morning at the acrobatic competition site. You can imagine Mr. Goat's joy! He went home and told his family how much he had learned from Mr. Spider and that he hoped to win something from the competition.

As planned, they met at the site the following day, and Mr. Spider kept remarkably close to Mr. Goat, so people thought what good friends they were. On the other hand, Mr. Spider had a cruel personal reason for being that close to Mr. Goat. Very soon, the competition started. Mr. Spider went with the group that took the opening show; he was a great acrobatic performer! However, Mr. Goat began to have cold feet after watching how good and excellent the others were, but Mr. Spider kept encouraging him to go and display his skills because he was as good as the others. As soon as the goat accepted the challenge, got into the acrobatic act, and turned upside down on the bar, God said: Mr. Goat, so you are the one who has been stealing my beautiful plantains from my farm; you have the magic tube in your anus.

Mr. Goat was so offended and ashamed that he immediately tried to defend himself. He was about to explain how the magic tube got into his anus when Mr. Spider stopped him because he did not want his name mentioned. He quickly threw sand into Mr. Goat's mouth, so he had to stop and clean the sand from his mouth. So he went, *Pii-pii, pii-pii*, and before he could say anything again, he was taken to God's house! So, Mr. Goat was not able to defend himself in public in front of everybody and explain that he was not the thief, but that it was Mr. Spider who stole the plantains. He was just an innocent victim of Mr. Spider's wicked tricks.

Mr. Spider tricked him into spending the night in his house to learn how to perform the acrobatic display. Mr. Goat also told God how Mr. Spider had asked him a day prior to the previous night to stay awake, and how he had forgotten and slept deeply; how Mr. Spider had treated him the following day for failing to stay awake. Furthermore, Mr. Goat explained to God how he had kept vigil the last night before the competition and how quickly he had jumped up to switch places with Mr. Spider, not knowing this was his intention. So that was how he ended up with the tube, by changing positions with Mr. Spider, thinking that he would receive some magical powers to help him with his acrobatic lessons.

Now, the result is that he has been accused of something that he would never have dreamt of doing, stealing God's plantain. Consequently, he was not even allowed to defend himself in front of the whole community because Mr. Spider again threw sand into his mouth, so he had to stop and clean the sand from his mouth. In the meantime, he was dragged into God's house with people hooting at him and calling him all kinds of names.

After Mr. Goat's arrest, Mr. Spider left town with his family that very night because he knew the consequences of what he had done to Mr. Goat and his family. When Almighty God heard the truth about the matter, he searched for Mr. Spider and his family, but they were nowhere to be found. They had already left town. This made everyone believe that it was not Mr. Goat but Mr. Spider who was the thief.

However, knowing the truth did not stop the feeling of disgrace and pain that Mr. Spider had inflicted upon the Goat family, but at least they were cleared of being thieves. Since Mr. Spider threw the sand into Mr. Goat's mouth, the goat has never stopped trying to clean the sand from his mouth.

That is why goats continue today to make that sound, *pii-pii, pii-pii*. They are still trying to get the sand out of their mouths. Stories like this instruct us how to learn not to fall into such cunning friends' company, and be wise when dealing with people because we never know the real intentions of others. How many individuals have fallen victim to such scams? A wise saying or proverb would be:

Cover yours up and open mine to the public.

A person's head is not like a pawpaw that one can open up and see inside!

It is through many friendships that the crab has no head!

When you are climbing a tree with a hypocritical individual, let them climb first!

The same cane used to flog Takyi would be used to flog Baah!

What's sauce for the goose is also sauce for the gander.

The tentacle of a fool is only stepped upon once!

The first fool is not a fool, but the second fool is a fool!

I have been beaten and forbidden to cry!

Have you made a fool of me and explained it to me?

THE KING AND THE FOOLISH SERVANT

Many, many years ago, there lived a king who was incredibly famous and wise. He had many servants who ran his affairs in his country while he ;led to other countries, settling serious matters for them. He paid his servants very well, so they all stayed with him and became like children to him. Among his servants was a very devoted Christian who took all the Christian teachings to heart and acted upon them even though his good deeds left him sometimes penniless. He would give it to everyone who asked him for help if he had it. Most of the time, his friends intentionally ask for help, knowing that he would help them and then not pay it back as promised.

This attitude went on for years until his friends called him foolish because he had never learned from what people were doing to him. He would defend himself by saying, "My reward is in heaven if that is what people are doing with my kindness of heart." Somehow the news reached his master, the king, who called the servant into his presence and asked if what he had been hearing about him was correct. He said it was proper that he helped all who were in need if he had it; if not, he did not worry about it. The master asked the servant if he had received back the money he gave out to others. And he answered that if they had the means, they would have paid him back.

The master was shocked to hear such an explanation from this hard-working servant, who was wasting his money on others who did not want to work. After recovering from his shock, the master took from under his garment a stick and gave it to the servant with these words: "You are the most foolish person I have come across. So keep this stick and pass it on to them when you find someone worse than you." The servant took the stick, left his master's presence without giving it a second thought, and continued to do what he had been doing: being kind and generous to those in need.

As years went by, his master began to show signs of age and could not travel as much as he used to when he was younger. When the time came for him to leave this world to return to his Creator, he was wise enough to call all of his servants to bid them farewell as the time drew near. When they all gathered around him, he told them that he knew he did not have a long time with them before he would have to leave on his journey, so he wanted to thank them for their years of service. Furthermore, he wanted to give them portions of his property worth their time with him, since they would not be able to go in search of new jobs at their age. He gave them enough to survive on until they died if they were wise in using it.

As soon as the master finished his reasons for inviting them to his bedside, the supposedly foolish servant, as he was known by then, asked his master if he had prepared himself for his journey. The master thought the foolish servant did not understand that he was dying and not talking about ordinary travel. So, the master explained that he did not need to pack any clothing where he was going. The servant asked again, Have you prepared yourself for your journey? At this point, the master was getting irritated with his lack of understanding that he was dying and said aloud that he was about to die. The foolish servant answered and said, "This is all the more reason that you need to prepare yourself to meet your Maker. During your earthly travels, you packed luggage when you traveled, but now that you are going to meet your Creator, you did not do so." As he was saying this, he pulled from under his cloak the stick his master had given him years ago and handed it over to him, saying, "You are the worst foolish man I have ever come across who never prepared his soul to meet his Maker. So here is your stick."

Not long after this, his master died. So, the stick the master gave to the servant for doing his Christian duty was returned to him on his dying bed. It became a lesson for the rest of the town that if you do not understand what someone else is doing, do not judge them harshly according to your own opinion or understanding of what they should be doing. This story is a good lesson for us today because we are quick to criticize people when we do not understand their intention for doing what they are doing. A wise saying or proverb would be:

One person's meat is another person's poison!

Kindness is its reward.

Patience moves mountains.

Whatever you do, people will talk about you.

If you think you know everything about hunting, you will catch nothing.

Problems do not find people; it is people who find problems!

Your wish was that the tree must fall on Kweku, but the tree has fallen on Kobina.

If you do good, you do it for yourself; and if you do bad, you do it for yourself!

THE REASON WHY GOD MOVED SO FAR AWAY FROM THE EARTH

An exceptionally long time ago, the earth and the sky were remarkably close together. The Almighty God lived close to us in the sky. On earth, there lived a toothless old woman who could not chew her food, so she decided to pound her plantain and cassava into fufu so that she could swallow them in small lumps.

Every evening she would take her mortar and pestle and pound her fufu, but in the process, she would hit the Almighty God with her pestle since the sky and the Earth were so close together. God started to complain to her about the situation, but the old woman did not pay any attention to the complaints. So finally, God decided to move further away from the Earth rather than stay and take the punishment every evening. So, off went God into the distance, where the pestle never reached again. So, God was happy, and the old woman was happy too, to be able to eat her fufu in peace. That is why God is so far away from the Earth today.

A story like this one will tell us, children, not to hurt one another because if we do, our friends or the people we are hurting may move away, and we may never see them again. Additional wisdom in this story would be how to solve a problem amicably, so each one involved would be happy and content, just like God and the old lady solved theirs.

Understanding brings peace!

Love creates understanding in a town.

Love your friend as yourself and love your neighbor as oneself.

Honesty and trust create harmony.

Sympathy is the key to adjustment for another person.

THE REASON WHY THE SHEEP GETS HIT MORE OFTEN BY A CAR THAN THE GOAT

Many years ago, all the domestic animals lived together in one place. The goat has always been extremely aggressive, and the sheep calm and collected by nature; one day, the two of them decided to travel together on an exceptionally long trip on which they had to take transportation to their destination. When they set off from the house, the sheep took enough money to pay its fare on the journey. The goat did not have enough money saved for the trip, but it did not ask for help or tell anyone about it, but decided not to pay when it rode on the vehicle to its destination.

Sure enough, as soon as they arrived, the driver's helper collected their fares. The goat slipped away, and the sheep paid its fare, but the man did not give her the change because he thought the sheep paid for the two of them, and the car drove away. Since then, the sheep has been waiting for its change from the driver, so when a vehicle is coming it will not move from the road, thinking it was the driver who took its balance away with him. On the other hand, as soon as the goat hears a car's horn, it will run away, thinking the driver will ask it for its unpaid fare. And that is the reason why the sheep gets hit by cars more often than the goat.

This kind of story is for entertainment, but there is also a great lesson to learn from this because sometimes we associate with people whose attitudes are like the goat who creates trouble wherever they go. Then we find ourselves in trouble because we are with them. So, a wise saying or a proverb that goes with a story like this would be:

Show me your friend, and I will tell you your character.

If one person acts disgracefully, it affects the whole village or town.

A bad character disgraces a person.

Association with bad company ruins one's character.

THE STORY ABOUT HOW GOD TESTED HIS THREE WIVES TO SEE WHO LOVED HIM THE MOST

A long time ago, God lived amongst the people of the Earth. God married three wives; the first was named Vulture, the second was called Frog, and the third and youngest was named Hen. They lived in a very wonderful village where they had farms and everything one could hope for, and the women were happy beyond words. They showed their affection toward their husband in many diverse ways. After many years, God started wondering if the affection the three women were showing was genuine or if it was because they had everything they could desire.

One day God came up with an idea to test them and see which one loved him the most; he told them he was not feeling well and after a short time, he pretended to die. So, he was laid in state for the wives to wail for their husband one by one, so the people would know how they would honor their husband.

As stories go, the people and the family arrange for the senior wife to wail first, followed by the middle and the youngest wife last. So, Vulture started from the end of the village where people had gathered and started singing:

I have always eaten from garbage while he was alive so if he is dead, it does not change much!

She sang and wailed throughout where the people had gathered and came to where God's body was laid and finished her time of wailing for her husband.

Then they asked the second, which was Frog, to start her wailing and so she also started:

I am going to divorce since my husband is dead. I am going to divorce since my husband is dead, Ama Ewisiwae I am dead! (Ama Ewisiwae was her name.)

She also went through the same places where Vulture went and came to where the body was laid in state and finished her turn of wailing.

So, they asked the youngest wife to go and wail for her husband, the same as the other two, and so she also prepared herself and started where the two women began and opened her mouth and sang:

Where must I go *Kwaa* (painful sound), where must I go? My husband is dead *Krokro* (another painful sound).

She also took the same path the two had taken and came to where the body was and to everyone's amazement, God got up and said, now I know who loves me and who is with me because they have their needs fulfilled.

So, God told Vulture to go and do what she said she was already doing through her wailing song; that is why vultures always eat from the garbage to this day.

God told Frog she would have her wish since her song indicated that she wanted a divorce, and sent her away by divorcing her.

All the people in the village and those who came knew from the way Hen wailed for her husband that she was the one who genuinely loved God the most. God asked her to always raise up her head for a blessing whenever she drinks water. And that is the reason why all chickens raise their heads when they drink water.

Such a story is entertaining, but it also shows how true honesty and dedication can be a blessing unawares. The reason I tell the hard truth comes from living with such stories day in and day out and hearing it from various sources wherever I went as a child. The wisdom or a proverb that should go with such a story would be:

Quality goods sell themselves!

When one gives a dedicated service, one's debts get forgiven!

Dedication, understanding, and true love make a marriage last longer.

Being too wise in your own eyes does not take one into good places.

Honesty is its own reward.

THE REASON WHY SPIDERS ARE FLAT

A very long time ago, spiders had bodies like humans, but it was through Mr. Spider's greed that he ended up flat and made his descendants all flat as well. Mr. Spider was a farmer and a good one at that, but he always wanted to have more than everyone else. So, he went to his farm very early in the morning and left very late in the evening so he would clear more land and harvest more crops. One day he had a new plot of land to clear, so he went early as usual. As soon as he started to weed, he heard a voice asking, Who is that? Mr. Spider answered very quickly it is just Mr. Spider trying to clear new land to plant his corn, and to his surprise, the voice said, Children, go and help Mr. Spider to weed his farm. And out of nowhere, many people appeared and helped him clear the whole land. He thanked them, and they disappeared, and he could not imagine his luck and how much they had weeded for him, as he would never have been able to do in several months by himself.

He returned home early, and his wife and children were surprised and asked him if anything had brought him home that early; he shared with them what had happened and that now they had more cleared land than they would ever have imagined. Being a good woman, the wife suggested that he be careful because the land might belong to a land god, who was kind enough to help him since he wanted to farm there. So, Mr. Spider waited for the weeded land to dry so he could burn it and prepare it for planting the corn; again, as soon as he got to the farm and hit his tool on the ground, the voice asked, Who is it? Mr. Spider was getting used to this and enjoying it very much, so he answered, It is Mr. Spider gathering the weeds together to burn and make the land ready for planting. And the voice said, Children, go and help Mr. Spider to gather the weeds and burn and prepare the land for planting. Again, out of nowhere appeared many people to finish the work in a very short time.

This time when Mr. Spider returned home early, his wife, Aso, knew why and there was no need to be surprised, so she just said, you got your helping hands today as well, which made Mr. Spider laugh. He waited for the first rain to fall and then went to the farm with his corn to plant; this time, he hit the ground very hard. And sure enough the voice as usual asked, Who is that? And Mr. Spider answered that it was him and he was planting his corn. The voice told the children to go and help him to plant, and within a very short time, the whole field was planted for Mr. Spider; he thanked them and left. When the corn germinated and needed to be weeded, Mr. Spider got the same help as usual. The farm was exceedingly beautiful and clean of weeds. Mr. Spider watched the corn stalks produce wonderful heavy ears of corn. So he decided to go away for some time because now he knew for sure that there was a benevolent land god who had been assisting him with his work. From now on, he must be careful what he did on the farm because he knew he would get help whatever work he did. Since the corn was not ready to be harvested, he decided to travel until the time came to harvest it. Before he left, he asked his wife and children not to go onto the farm until he returned, but when Aso, his wife asked if it was alright to go and collect some firewood from there, Mr. Spider said it was alright.

A week after Mr. Spider was gone, the family ran out of firewood, so Aso carried her young son on her back and went to the farm to collect some firewood. As soon as the boy saw the corn, he started crying and would not stop worrying about his mother getting him one ear of corn. To quiet the boy and collect her firewood, she decided to gently break off one ear of corn and give it to him to keep him quiet; but as soon as she broke the ear of corn, the voice came out, Who is that? And since she could not lie, she said, It is

I, Aso, Mr. Spider's wife who broke off an ear of corn to give to my son to keep him quiet. To her utter surprise, the voice said, Children, go and help Aso to break more corn to keep her son quiet; within a few minutes, the whole corn farm had been harvested, and they were not even ready to be eaten and to dry them for cornmeal. Aso came home a dejected woman and did not know what to do but had to wait for her husband to return so she could tell him about the tragic story.

As it happened, Mr. Spider did not come home first. Since he was curious about how his corn farm had fared, he went there the first two days after the incident had happened. When he saw how the whole corn crop was cut down, and the corn was not even ready to be eaten, he hit his chest to say whoever had done that would pay dearly for it. The voice asked, Who is this? And Mr. Spider answered and said, I was so shocked that all of the corn had been wasted that I hit my chest in desperation. The voice said, Children, go and help Mr. Spider to beat his chest in sorrow. Out of nowhere, the multitude appeared and started hitting Mr. Spider's chest; by the time they finished, they had flattened Mr. Spider as thin as they could, and Mr. Spider jumped and hid behind a leaf. And that is why Spiders are flat, even though from the beginning of creation, they were not flat like that. That is also why you find them in the bush with their web built from one tree to the next; they are still hiding from the children who beat Mr. Spider's chest until he was flattened like that. This story is for entertainment, but it also has many lessons to learn from it. So, the wise sayings and proverbs that could go with this would be:

Hastily acquired, hastily lost!

Greediness leads to death.

Receiving greedily may end in death.

Had I known is always too late.

If wisdom were for sale, then only rich people would be wise! (With all the prior encounters and events, Mr. Spider never learned.)

All sweet events have some bitter sides to them.

Sometimes the bitter medicine cures people faster.

Advice does not change a person faster than a bitter experience does.

THE REASON WHY PEOPLE ARE ADVISED TO TAKE GOOD CARE OF ORPHANS

A very long time ago there lived in a town a very assiduous man whom everyone loved and admired. He married two wives; the first wife had four children named Kutukutu, Kwaakwaa, Kwaakwaa-nyako, and Dzeaonyibi; but the younger wife only had one daughter named Danso. However, they were happy as a family, or so it seemed, until suddenly the younger wife died and left Danso with her rival. The husband was devastated because he loved both of his wives dearly; after the burial and funeral ceremonies were over, all the family members returned to their various places, including Danso's maternal grandmother. As soon as everyone was gone, and the husband was busy with his work, the stepmother started treating Danso badly; she asked her to do most of the work in the house, and then when it came to the distribution of food, she would divide it in such a way so that poor Danso would not have any. She would sing out the names of her children to come and pick up their food. Then she put her mother-in-law, the husband, and herself on the side and then sang that there was not enough food for Danso to get a share, so Danso must sit on the side. This is the song she would sing when she was distributing the food:

Here is Kutukutu's food,
Here is Kwaakwaa's food,
Here is Kwaakwaa-nyako's food,
Here is Dzeaonyibi's food,
Here is my in-law's food,
Here is my husband's food,
Here is food for me.
But the food was not enough for Danso to get some; so Danso get up and sit on the side.

So, Danso could not eat but just sit on the side and watch them as most of them ate, except that the husband and his mother will eat later. This went on for a long time, so Danso started showing signs of not being well cared for; at first, everyone assumed it was because of her mother's death, not knowing she was being starved by her stepmother. And not knowing that the ghost of Danso's mother had been watching all this time. So one day, the ghost could not stand it any longer because she thought her husband would investigate why Danso was getting very thin and looking uncared for, but he was just into his work and not paying much attention to her only daughter.

So, the ghost came to the house one day when the rival was distributing the food as usual. As soon as the first wife finished her song and the distribution of the food and asked Danso to go and sit on the side, the ghost appeared and immediately started singing:

Kutukutu dies today,
Kwaakwaa dies today,
Kwaakwaa-nyako dies today,
Dzeaonyibi dies today,
My in-law dies today,
My husband dies today,
My rival dies today,
My daughter Danso, death, and food have passed over you so pick up yourself and sit on the side.

Immediately the whole household died because as soon as their names were mentioned in the song, they fell dead, including the husband and mother-in-law, who were not physically present where the food was being distributed. Danso was the only one spared. So she ran out and called out to lots of people to come and see what was happening in their house. When they came and found them all dead, Danso narrated to them what had been going on since her mother died and was buried, and the families went back to their various homes. Afterward, everyone said they thought Danso was getting thinner because she was still grieving her mother, not knowing that she was not being fed.

So, the village Chief made a rule that everyone must pay more attention to an orphan because they did not have anywhere else to go and get help if the family refused to care for them. And if they refused to do so, as Danso's stepmother did, the dead mother's ghost will come and kill them too. So, it is up till this day that in most cultures, orphans are cared for with love and great attention!

A story like this would be told to make one aware that being an orphan is already a sad situation, so people must be kind to a motherless child! A wise saying or proverb to go with such a story would be:

Your clan comes to an end when your mother dies.

Even if the back of your hand tastes good, it will never be like the palm of your hand.

It is only a parent who knows how their children will eat.

Only a mother knows how to care for her bad child.

Rivalry is like cow dung: when the top is dried, then the bottom is very wet!

Death destroys many things.

Death destroys family.

An orphan's life is very sad!

THE REASON WHY THE LAND
CROCODILE MAMPAM IS DEAF

Many many years ago, all the animals lived together, including the flying insects. They decided to elect a king who would arbitrate between them when there was a misunderstanding, and so they elected the land crocodile called Mampam in the Ghanaian language. He was truly a very good and kind ruler, settling many problems between the animals. Until one day came when he had dealt with so many problems that he had had enough of being a king. He thought he had finished for the day when suddenly a knock was heard at his door. When he responded, there were mosquito and frog who had had an encounter that they wanted the king to hear about and help them settle. The mosquito accused the frog of giving him cheek when he asked her an important question as she returned from the market.

When Mampam asked the mosquito to tell him what happened, he said that when the frog came from the market, she had to cross a river, and he wanted to know if, with the recent rain, the river had risen; the frog said yes, the river had risen so much that it was up to her knees. Mosquito replied that he wanted to know how the frog could tell the water had risen so much, but just to her knees. That was a cheek to him, and that was why he brought the frog to the king's house so the king would find out what the frog meant.

King Mampam asked the frog if she had heard what the mosquito had said, and what does she have to say about it? So, the frog said to the king, that it was true, that was what she answered the mosquito, and it was not a cheek. But if he thinks so, she has a complaint against the mosquito. Because a week ago, she did not go to the market, but the mosquito went, and she asked him after his return if there were yams and if the yams were suitable sizes. The mosquito answered her that yes, there were plenty of yams, and they were as large as his thigh. The frog did not say anything but thanked him; now she wants to know if the king thinks that was a cheek he gave her because she could ask a similar question of the mosquito: how big is he that he could compare a large yam to his thigh?

After hearing the frog's answer, the king was even more perplexed about what to say. So he sent them both away from his presence and decided he had had enough with hearing such nonsense, and he did not want to hear anything like that again. So he put sticks in his ears and blocked his hearing, from that day on he has been deaf. When people want to catch a Mampam, they will make loud noises, and it will stay there until they catch it; but if they talk in undertones, it will hear and run away.

A story like this is for entertainment but also has some teaching and wisdom; sometimes others can pressure you so much that you may do something dreadful to yourself as a result. We see this in our societies these days: how people are destroying themselves in many ways because of the pressures others put on them. A proverb or wise saying that will go with such a story would be:

If taking a position will make you suffer, it is better to be an ordinary common member of society.

Do not envy somebody's position because it may not be worth much.

Silly questions deserve silly answers.

Every pot has its own cover!

When you know you are guilty, you do not take your case to court.

Courts were built because of cheating.

THE STORY OF A TRADITIONAL PRIEST WHO SAID WHEN HE SPEAKS, NOBODY CONTRADICTS HIM!

A very long time ago, there lived in a village a traditional priest (Okomfo) who was granted so much wisdom that he believed that nobody could contradict him whatever he said. His fame spread far and wide so that people invited him to come to their places to solve problems or help find things out for them. As we all know, some people did not believe he knew that much and that he was faking most of the time. He had one daughter named Esi Maame that he traveled around with, and she was very smart and friendly, so she made friends easily when she went into a new town or village.

As time passed, the traditional priest was invited to a town called Asebu to identify the king of that town among several kings who would be in the large group. And so a date was set, and when the time came, a large crowd gathered like a durbar to witness what this traditional priest could do. As usual, many spectators from other towns and villages came to witness such a remarkable feat of this traditional priest's powers of wisdom and knowing secrets. The event was supposed to last from morning until six o'clock in the evening, and if he were able, he would be honored with several gifts; but if he failed, he would be executed since he would have been lying to the people.

The father and daughter arrived in town the day before the event to rest and prepare themselves for the great event. As usual, the daughter went through the town and just listened to the stories as she tried to make friends and also become familiar with the place; as she went out, she heard many accounts. Including how she could help her father to identify the King of Asebu. She heard someone say the king would not dress in his kingly robes with the rest of the kings but would dress as an ordinary person wearing a blanket hat. She also heard important information that the king would dress like a woman and not only have two breasts but four; and that he would be wearing a hat made from a blanket, just to disguise himself. So, since they danced together when such things were being accomplished, she would be able to assist her father in achieving his task if she noticed the father had no clue how to find the king of Asebu by himself.

The festivities began right on time, and hundreds, and hundreds of people showed up, including enough kings and queens to confuse anybody as they arrived in droves to take their seats. Esi was watching for only one character as she heard yesterday when she strolled through town. Sure enough, closer to the end of the arrival time, the King of Asebu arrived just as was described and did not sit where the kings and queens were but sat amongst the ordinary people.

The time came to introduce the traditional priest to the gathering, and those who knew him before started making loud noises calling his name out, "When you say nobody contradicts you," and the party began in earnest; there was drumming and dancing, and the priest and daughter were dancing and singing as they went around amongst the gathering. The time was going fast, and when the father realized he could not find the king amongst so many, and the day was moving towards evening, he started singing to his daughter, asking for help, and he began to sing this way:

Priest: Esi maame
Girl: Yes, my father
Priest: I have not been able to identify him

Girl: Look at the person dressed up with three or four breasts wearing a blanket hat; I tell you that is the King of Asebu. My father, learning is a good thing because the time is almost up!

They repeated the question and answers in song repeatedly and the time was getting late. When they were near where the King of Asebu was sitting, the daughter danced closer to her father and pushed him so that he fell into the lap of the Asebu king, and quickly held his hands up to indicate to the multitudes that that was the King of Asebu.

The crowd came and picked the traditional priest up as well as the King of Asebu, and there was such great joy and jubilation that the gathering did not end so soon that people would have been disappointed but was allowed to have a full day of celebration before the right king was shown to the public. So, they honored the traditional priest and his daughter as they promised and even more that he was right when he says nobody contradicts him!

The traditional priest thanked his daughter for being the one who solved the problem for him today, and all the honor is due to her and not to him because, without her, things would have gone wrong for him since he never dreamt of the Asebu king would disfigure himself like that; so he was not even looking at that person at all until she danced and pushed him into his lap. The daughter was happy that she could help save her father from a disgraceful death because it would have reflected upon her, too if he had been killed.

A story like this is purely for entertainment, but it still has some learning and wisdom in it, and so the proverb or the wise saying to go with it would be:

When two set a trap together, it takes both to visit it.

The cup used to draw water is always wet.

When someone says you look like your parents, do not hastily laugh.

If one sheep gets sick, it affects the whole herd.

It is because of needs, that is why animals walk in twos.

If someone beats you until you go to the toilet, it would not be the same as when you must go.

One head does not take council; two heads are better than one.

THE MAN WHO PLANTED A GOLDEN
APPLE IN HIS GARDEN

A very long time ago, a man named Kwesi Mensa, and his family planted a beautiful garden with an apple tree in the garden. For many years the apple tree would not produce any apples, but one year the family suddenly saw blossoms on the apple tree, and they were so pleased to see it finally come of age. To everyone's surprise, the apple tree bore only three fruits, and they were golden apples. They watched those golden apples getting bigger and bigger, and one day they noted that the three golden apples were about ready to be picked. So, the man asked his three sons, Kofi, Kweku, and Kojo, to take turns guarding the apples day and night. So, Kofi, the senior son, decided to keep watch the first night and stay awake until the morning and then sleep during the day. Kweku, the second son, will follow next, and last of all, Kojo, their younger brother. Everyone agreed to the arrangement, so the older brother Kofi was to watch for the first night. He prepared himself and took whatever was necessary for the night with him, including his gun, so anybody who attempted to come and steal any of the apples would be shot!

Unfortunately, Kofi waited and waited, and since nobody was coming to the garden, he slept. To his horror, one of the three golden apples was gone when he woke up in the morning. This was unacceptable to him. Who would have come to climb the apple tree without any noise? Yet one of the golden apples was gone. This made Kweku, the middle brother, anxious and determined to be very careful; he also took what he thought necessary to help him stay awake and see who would come and steal the golden apple. Well, guess what? Another golden apple was gone by the time he woke up from sleep under the apple tree.

Now, there was a mystery in town to solve, because two golden apples had been stolen with someone watching and sleeping under the apple tree. Now it was Kojo, the youngest brother's turn to go and keep watch, so he took everything he wanted and was so imaginative that he decided to take some sewing pins and put them on the back of the chair he would sit on and watch. So when sleep overtook him, his head would hit the back of the chair, waking him up.

He was right, he could not resist sleeping, but when he did doze off, his head hit on the pins and woke him up. This went on for a while, and when closer to midnight, he suddenly saw a bright light coming from a distance, which woke him up. And sure enough, a giant bird came right to the apple tree and plucked the last apple. Even though Kojo gave it a good bang, he could not kill it, although one of its feathers fell to the ground. Wonders never cease because the feather was a golden feather, and so Kojo waited. In the morning, when the family and others gathered around him. He showed them the feather and told the story of how a golden bird picked the golden apples. They carried the golden feather home. The father said they had to find where that golden bird came from and bring back the golden apples.

Again, Kofi, the senior brother, was to set out first to search for the golden bird, and he was provided with enough provisions and a horse for his journey. As soon as he set out, he began following where people had shared stories about where they heard people talk about the golden bird, a golden horse, and a golden person they had encountered on their journeys. He did not go too far on his journey before he met a fox, and the fox begged him for some food, but he was not kind to it and told the fox he did not know where he was going and did not know if he would have enough food to last him for his journey, so how can he give him some food. However, the fox told him he was on the right path, but it was going to be a long, tempting journey, so he better be careful. His first temptation will soon be upon him because there is an enchanted village ahead. If he takes any drinks in that town, that will be the end of his journey.

The fox disappeared as soon as he offered him that information. It was not long before he came to that village with all kinds of music and drinks. He was, of course, alone, tired, and wanted something to cheer him up. As soon as he tasted the drinks, he forgot what he was searching for and stayed there in the village.

After many months of hearing nothing from him, the second brother Kweku decided to go and try his luck and prepare for his long journey. As soon as he set out, the same fox met him and also asked for some food. He refused to give it any, and the fox gave him the same information he gave to his senior brother Kofi. However, when Kweku reached the town, and his older brother met him, it was easy to stop and join him for some fun. But as soon as he did that, his journey ended there.

The family waited for several months and said to the younger son Kojo that since it was he who was able to shoot the bird, maybe he would be the one to find the bird and come back, and so he must get ready to go in search of the bird and maybe his brothers as well. So, Kojo also got ready and prepared himself with whatever he thought he might need on the journey, and the day came for him to depart; the townspeople came and bid him farewell and good luck, and so he left his town and set off for the task ahead of him. Kojo did not go too far on the road when the same fox met him and asked him for some food. Kojo got off his horse and fed the fox and played with the fox a little before he was about to start again when to his surprise, the fox started talking to him about what was ahead and where his brothers had failed to pass the first village that led to where they could have found what they went out in search of to find. So he must resist passing through the town with all his might because his brothers would try to dissuade him from succeeding where they had failed.

He thanked the fox and continued his journey. Sure enough, in a few hours, he came to the village, and his brothers were the first to come to him before anybody else, saying that he must rest, and they would go with him if he did. But he refused, even though they were forcing drinks on him while riding on his horse. The horse was able to get through the village with him, and to his surprise, as soon as they passed through the town, there was the same fox again, waiting for him on the other side. The fox told him many things ahead of him that he would come to and explained to Kojo that if he listened carefully, he would get what he went in search of—plus many other things he did not know existed. So Kojo thanked the fox and shared a meal with it, and when he was ready, the fox reminded him that he was going to enter a town where there was a golden horse that soldiers guarded. He must walk straight to where the horse is kept and untie it. And within the stable, he would find two horse whips: one made of gold, and one made of ordinary leather. He must use only the ordinary whip to get the golden horse out of the stable, and nothing will happen. But if he touches the horse with the golden whip, the horse will neigh, and he would be arrested.

Kojo soon entered the town and did as the fox had told him and almost got out, but as always happens in such stories, he touched the horse with the golden whip, and the horse neighed so loudly that in a second, he found himself surrounded by soldiers. They asked him where he was going with the horse, and he said that his father had one that he played with, so he was just playing with it and not going anywhere with it. He was told that if he wanted to go free, he must go into the next town where there was a golden human, and bring him to them, then they would give him the golden horse. And with a few slaps, he was sent off to the next town. Not long after he crossed the outskirts of the town, the fox appeared and asked him why he had made that mistake. He was lucky that he did not get himself killed but instead had been sent on another adventure. And so the fox told him where the golden human was and how to get there. He warned him that a giant guards the golden man and that he must be cautious, or the giant would kill him. All he must do is step into the house where the golden man was and ask him to follow him, and he will get up and follow him.

Kojo did as he was told. However, when the golden man got up and followed him, he thought he needed to tell someone before they walked outside the town, or he would be arrested for stealing. So he turned back and told someone that he would play with the golden man for a while. When he was arrested and brought to the king, he explained that he was not stealing the golden man but was going to play with him. And then pointed out that if he had wanted to rob him, he would not have told anyone. The king agreed and told Kojo that if he wanted to play with the golden man, he must go to the next town and bring him the golden bird before he could play with the golden man.

Again, the fox met Kojo, pleaded with him not to be so careless with his life, and showed him where the golden bird was. He also told him that the golden bird has two nests: one was gold, and the second one was ordinary. And just like the horse, if he put the bird in the common nest, he could get away with it, but if he put it in the golden one, the bird would cry out and set off an alarm so that he would be arrested. Kojo soon got there and saw the three golden apples near its nests, and he knew he had found the right bird who came and took their golden apples from their tree. The bird was already in the ordinary nest, but he saw how beautiful the golden perch was. Kojo picked it up and put it in the golden nest. As soon as he did, such a cry brought everyone to where the bird was, and there he was also, caught red-handed, holding the golden bird in his hand. He was quickly arrested, imprisoned, and given an impossible task to perform in a month or face death.

Kojo was then ordered to clear a massive mountain by himself. If he succeeded, what he told the king was the truth, and he would be given the golden bird. But if he failed, that proved that he had lied, and he would be killed. Even though Kojo went out every day and worked until late in the evening, very little got accomplished. The days turned into weeks; before he realized it, the month was ending, and only a little dent had been made in the mountain. On the last day, he went out, knowing that he would be killed no matter what. So he just sat and thought about his home, family, and friends and especially about his two brothers who will never be set free so they can go home to their parents; he also thought about how he had disappointed his good friend, the fox. As it was getting closer to the time for him to return to his prison cell, his friend the fox appeared, sat by his side, and started telling him how he had suffered all that pain because of his carelessness. Kojo told the fox how sorry he was now, knowing that he had wasted all his help in vain, but the fox said there was still hope for him.

The fox asked Kojo to wait for him, and he would be back; sure enough, the fox returned with three leaves in its mouth, put them on the vast mountain, and then stood up and hit the leaves with its tail, and the mountain disappeared! You should have seen the look on Kojo's face. The fox then instructed him to go back into his cell as he had done every day and wait for the morning of his execution when they would come and call him and ask if he had finished his work. Then he could tell them yes, and for the king to go and see so he could get his golden bird and its two nests.

Kojo did as he was told, and when morning came, he did not wake up on time, and people thought it was because he was going to be killed. This was why he had not gotten up. They went and woke him up when it was time to talk. When they asked if he had finished his work, he said yes and that they must summon the king to come and inspect his work and give him his golden bird with its two nests. The news soon reached the king and spread quickly. The whole town went out to look, and to their surprise, the mountain was gone, and they could see a city further away that they had never seen before. The king was true to his word and gave Kojo the golden bird with its two nests. Kojo took the golden bird and the two nests and set out on his way to the town where the golden man was. The fox met and congratulated him, and Kojo also thanked the fox for saving his life and being his companion on his journey in search of this golden bird.

Kojo arrived safely where the golden man was, and when the people saw him back with the golden bird, they were amazed and happy that they were going to trade the golden man for the golden bird, which would lay golden eggs for them. However, the young man said he would like to see how good it looked, with the golden man holding the golden bird in his hands and riding with them to see if he wanted to trade. And so they all agreed, and Kojo put the golden man on his horse and gave him the golden bird, and they all started riding around the open area where the people had gathered. The people were happy and excited to watch them, but on their third time around, Kojo took off from the town as fast as he could go on his horse. When the people realized they had been tricked, they ran after Kojo and tried to catch him, but soon lost him and had to return to town.

As he got closer to the next town, his friend the fox again appeared and congratulated him for what he had achieved. Kojo went straight to the city where the golden horse was; when the people there saw him come back with not only the golden man but also the golden bird, the town went wild with amazement and happiness to meet him and get the golden man in exchange for the golden horse. Kojo used the same trick with them, saying he wanted to ride the golden horse holding the golden bird with the golden man on it and see how he liked it before trading or exchanging the golden man. They readily agreed, so he took the golden horse and its two whips and sent his horse ahead while they were busy admiring the beauty of the golden horse being ridden with the golden man holding the golden bird in his hands. The third time around, just as before, Kojo took off as fast as he could ride. Since no horse could match the golden horse in speed, he ended up with all three gifts on his way home.

The fox met him as usual and told him what was ahead of him: that his brothers Kofi and Kweku would try to stop him from being successful with his search and warned him to be very careful. He told the fox that he would take his brothers home with him, if possible, now that he had two horses, but again, the fox warned him that it would not be easy. True to his word, when Kojo arrived on his golden horse at the place where his brothers were, he asked them to sit on his old horse before he could taste anything. And when they did, he rode with them out of that town. When they had gone some distance from that village, Kojo was so tired after his ordeals that he decided to rest. As soon as the brothers realized he was asleep, they tied him up and threw him into a pit and took all he had gained, and returned to the enchanted village; when they got there, they set watch on the road so in case he got out and was coming to the town for them, he could be killed. However, after they arrived, the golden horse would not eat, the golden man sat as though he was dead, and the golden bird put its head under its wings; for days, the brothers tried all they could, but nothing changed; they knew things were not going to go well for the man, the horse, and the bird in the village, but they were not willing to do anything about it, since they were powerless in that environment.

When Kofi and Kweku left their little brother Kojo to die in the pit, the fox came and, once again, stretched its tail until it reached the bottom of the hole and asked him to hold on to its rear; he was afraid to hurt his friend, but the fox encouraged him to hold on strong and tight so it could pull him out. So Kojo did, and out it pulled him and also healed his wounds from falling into the pit and also where they tied him up. The fox told him what his brothers had done and that they had hired people to kill him in case he got out and was coming after them, so he needed to disguise himself or he would not reach the village. Kojo saw a shepherd, exchanged clothes with him, and told him not to worry because he would take the sheep to the town, sell them for him, and bring his money back. The shepherd agreed and was happy to get a break for the day. And so it was that the young man returned to the enchanted village as a shepherd selling his sheep.

However, even before he started toward the village, the golden horse started eating its hay, the golden bird started singing, and the golden man perked up, but no one noticed. Kojo soon arrived and sold all the sheep, after which he collected his gains, tied up his brothers, put them on the second horse, and took them home. When he arrived with his gains and his captive brothers, the whole town gave him a welcome that had never been seen in the town before. Kojo wisely gave much credit for his success to the fox who befriended him and helped him on his journey; without the kind fox, he said, he would not have been able to succeed and would instead have failed like his brothers before him. He also stressed the importance of kindness, which began his friendship with the fox. Because if he had refused to share his meal with the hungry fox, the fox would not have helped him as he did; that opened up his brothers to admit their unkindness in refusing to allow the same fox who appeared to them for help. Unlike Kojo, they denied him food, so even though the fox shared the same information about the village, they failed to get through it.

A few months after their return, when things were returning to normal, the youngest brother decided to go to the bush for a bit of hunting; he did not go far in the bush when his friend the fox showed up, and they were happy indeed to see each other. So they talked for a while, and when the young man was about to ask permission to leave, the fox said that he needed his help. Kojo said, anything I can do to help you, I will do it. The fox warned him that what he was asking would be challenging, but he needed to do it for him and not worry about anything else. And Kojo did promise to do it for him. The fox asks the young man to go and collect three leaves from a medicinal tree called "Down hataa" in the Ghanaian language and bring them to him, and then he will tell him the next step. When he did, the fox told Kojo to put the three leaves on him, take a big stick, and beat him very hard. At this, the fox saw that Kojo's countenance had changed, but he pleaded, "if you love me," then you have to do it because if you do not. Who else will help me? Kojo replied that it was a tough request after all you have done for me, but if that is something that will help, I will do it with all my heart.

So the fox laid down, and the three leaves were put on him, and Kojo picked up the stick and started beating him. When the fox looked almost as if it were going to die, something strange happened. The fox turned into a beautiful man and said, you have achieved your goal; so you can stop. And Kojo threw the stick away and helped the other young man get up, and they hugged each other for a long time. Then Kojo asked him to tell him his story and why he became a fox because he always saw in him more than just a fox, even the first time they met on the roadside.

The Fox asked Kojo if he wanted to go hunting first, but Kojo said, No, he wanted to take him home to show him to his family first, and the hunting could wait. So, the two young men went home, and when people saw the two young men coming, they could tell there was some story to be told since they looked so happy together as though they had known each other all their lives.

As soon as they arrived at the house and the introduction was made. The parents said to wait and get the chief's attention before they went on with their stories; that was done. The chief summoned all the villagers into his palace and asked the family and the two young men to share what they had to say.

Kojo started with the story they all had become a part of, about the golden apple and how it took all three brothers out of the village in their quest. And finding the bird that came and plucked all their apples continued until he came to the part where he had to set off because his two brothers had not returned. And when he came, he told them how he had met a friendly fox who had helped him throughout his journey, and without his help, he would not have succeeded, just like his two brothers.

Then he continued with that very morning's encounter with the same fox again in the bush and how the fox had told him it needed his help now; and how he had almost not agreed to do what he asked him to do but because the fox said, "if he loved him," then he had to do it to help him. As he did it, the young man that emerged from the fox was whom they were looking at in front of them. At this, everyone was rejoicing and, simultaneously, weeping because it was hard to understand. The chief signaled for total silence and asked the new young man to proceed to tell his story.

He stood up and thanked the chief, his elders, and the people of the village for welcoming him into their midst with such love and said that he did not know how he would thank them in return. Then he told them that he was a king, and his stool name was Nana Atakora, but that a wicked magician had turned him into a fox because the magician wanted someone else to become king that he could manipulate and let him do his will. The whole place shouted with one accord, including the chief and his elders: "Live forever, oh King," and a kind king at that, who has helped one of our members to bring home such gifts that we did not know existed!

The young king said he had tried through several others to get the help he needed to return to his former self, but none of them was found worthy, except the one in front of the whole assembly. And so Nana Atakora, who was the former king of the three villages that owned the golden horse, man, and bird, said he wanted to take Kojo as his brother and that he did not need to return to his kingdom because the golden treasures that set them apart are now in this village. He was glad one of their members was able to take them away and bring them to where they were needed. He got the golden man, horse, and bird into existence during his father's reign. But now that they are all three with the one worthy of them, he would like to live here with them if they accepted him.

The chief and his elders consulted with the village members, and they all agreed to accept Nana Atakora as a village member. You can imagine the celebration that happened in that village. The chief and his elders proclaimed that from that day onward, any person who refused to be kind to any animal or human in need would be dealt with according to the law, because it was through kindness that the village had received such blessings as they have now.

So, the new addition brought all the wisdom he had to bear on the village's welfare and development; he married a woman from the village and raised several wonderful children, and they all lived happily ever after for many generations. Their story was shared with every generation so they would live with love and kindness as part of their lives and motto as a people. Such a story can be told to help young people learn how to show compassion and love, not knowing whom they may be kind to and the result their kindness will bring into the community. Proverbs and wise sayings that go with such a story will be:

When you do good for another, you also do it for yourself.

Sympathy takes one to a good place.

When huge events happen, they do not have a flag on them.

Kindness reaps good credits.

One reaps what one sows.

A bad character always dismisses the individual.

Helpers are scarce!

Prosperity comes from God!

What God has ordained cannot be thwarted!

Stubbornness does not benefit anybody.

The cane that was used in beating Takyi is the same one that is used for Baa.

Kind treatment shown to one person must be the same for the other.

Sauce for the goose is also sauce for the gander.

THE STORY OF A KING'S SON WHO COULD NOT BE CONSOLED AFTER HIS BEST FRIEND DIED

A very long time ago, there lived a king who had an only son named Bediako. Bediako had a bosom friend from childhood named Mempeasem; the two had become inseparable, and everyone in the town loved those boys and watched them grow up to become beautiful young men. They shared things and were as though they were born to the same parents.

As men, they trusted each other and were the talk of the town because even twins could not have been that close; they went everywhere as a pair, and you would not see one without the other. They spent their free time hunting game, and the king was so happy for his son since he was his only child, but now it seemed that the king had gained another son through his son's friendship with Mempeasem.

One day the unexpected happened: Mempeasem became very ill. Bediako would not leave his side until his final breath, and when this happened, everyone thought Bediako would die too.

His father was distraught and asked the elders to think of a way to help his son with his grieving. So, they tried to find out what made his friendship with Mempeasem so unique that no one else could fulfill that for him. When they asked him, Bediako said it was his friend's trust and honesty and that he believed no one else would ever have that kind of ability like the late Mempeasem. One of the elders told him that he could give him a friend who would be even more trusted than his late friend, in the person of Sunkwa; Bediako said he did not believe so, but he would give him a try and see.

The elders reported back to the king, and the king was relieved that something could be done to help his son with his grieving and loneliness. Not long after that, the elder who promised to bring the young man Sunkwa came to visit, and sure enough, he had a man almost Bediako's age, and he told the king that this was the person he promised Bediako would become his new friend. The king called his son into the room and introduced the other young man to him, and they agreed to try to become friends.

They were getting along well for several months when Bediako decided to test his new friend and see how trustworthy he was since the elder said he would be even better than his late friend Mempeasem. So Bediako went to the bush and hunted a deer and then dug a grave in the forest and laid banana branches in the freshly dug grave and put the large deer inside and then covered it. Bediako went home and was very quiet and was mourning when his friend Sunkwa came to find him, and as a friend wanted to know what had happened to put him in that mood again.

Bediako told his friend that he had accidentally killed a man when he went into the bush to hunt. Afterward, he was so afraid that he buried the man in the forest. So his new friend asked him to go and show him where this happened. And so he took him to the forest to where the grave was, and as soon as Sunkwa saw the blood on the soil, he knew that what Bediako had told him was true. Bediako then told his friend not to tell anyone about his accident and agreed that he would not tell anybody. So they went home together, sat, and visited for a while before Sunkwa left for his house.

He first told his father, and his father asked him to report it to the police station. And so they went together to report the case, and soon there was a knock on the palace door. When the king answered, the police told him his son had committed murder and buried the victim in the forest, so they were there to arrest him. The surprised king called his son, and the police asked his friend Sunkwa if he was that man, and Sunkwa said yes. And so the police took him away, and the king followed his son to the police station. The son said he did not know what they were talking about, so the police and the townspeople followed Sunkwa to the forest where the grave was, and everyone thought they had a murderer in their midst. So they started removing the soil from the grave, and as they did, Bediako just sat there weeping for his old friend, the late Mempeasem.

All kinds of nasty words were being used against Bediako until they got closer to the banana branches, removed them, and discovered a large deer had been killed. Its throat was cut, and the deer was buried in the supposedly dead man's grave. When the police pulled the deer out from the grave, the whole town started screaming unkind words at the elder and his son Sunkwa for what they had done to the good king and his worthy son by not knowing the truth and disgracing Bediako.

Sunkwa did not know what to say, only that when he saw the blood on the mud, he believed it was confirmed that Bediako had killed somebody by accident and buried him for sure; the people then asked him why he did not then inform the king rather than the police? And he said that his father encouraged him to make the report so that the police would not charge him with concealment of the body if the crime came out. After hearing that, he became terrified, and so did what his father suggested.

The police then charged Sunkwa with making a false report, causing the police to spend not only time but also money investigating a false allegation; the king and his son turned around and pleaded for him, insisting that the charge must be dropped because if he the king had not asked the elders to help his grieving son, all this would not have happened. And so Sunkwa should be allowed to go free. All of the town's people thanked the king and his son Bediako for their kindness and understanding; for now, they knew that people are hard to come by who are truly honest and trustworthy.

Such stories are told mainly for advice because it warns one not to share what is essential with friends. Some friends would betray you for their interest or bring your good name down, especially if you are someone important and they are jealous of your position. The following wise sayings and proverbs will go with such a story:

When you shake the rose tree, its smell will come out.

A true friend is more precious than gold or silver!

Only a fool says they mean my friend but not me.

When you see someone's beard burning, put water by yours.

When hypocrites live in a town, there is no peace in that town.

If you do not stop involving yourself in problems, you will not also have peace.

When people take time to communicate with each other, it clears confusion.

A case that will be settled peacefully always has a good intervener.

If a naked person promises to give you a cloth, just listen to their name.

If you have no money to purchase the goods, you just must return them to the owner!

An Akan person does not deserve a disgrace!

When the trap finally catches a too-known bird, it catches it by the neck!

A thief is caught by the hand and not by the leg!

A frog's length is only seen when it is dead!

A wound given by a word is more complicated to cure than that provided by a sword.

THE TWIN BROTHER KOBINA ATA KAKRA AND THE TWO-HEADED WOMAN

A very long time ago, there lived in a village a woman who had twin boys called Kobina Ata, and from their very early age, everyone could see the boys had extraordinary talents. As they grew, it became the talk of the village that those boys could do great things in the future, especially the younger twin Kobina Ata Kakra. He was talented with his bow, arrow, and guns and traveled to distant places with his horse. Whenever he got into trouble, his twin Kobina Ata Penyin would suddenly appear and be there for him. So, adventure became synonymous with Kakra; nobody knew when he would return home until he showed up. He liked to explore distant places, especially in the forests, for days on end. And he was never afraid of anything because he could change into so many things when he encountered problems and return home safely. At first, his mother was worried about him, but as he matured, his mother realized that he was an adventurer and accepted that.

One day during his wanderings, he went deep into the forest and saw a woman with two heads feeding both her heads. While one mouth was being fed, the other would say, "It is my turn, It is my turn," until it was fed, and so on, back, and forth. Kakra watched her for a while, then he cleared his throat, and the two heads became one, and the woman asked him if he saw anything. He said, No, I just got here. And the woman said, If you are not telling me the truth but lying, and if you go out and say anything about me, no matter where you are, I will come after you. So, they visited for a while, and then he said farewell, left, continued his journey, and finally returned home to his village as he always did.

However, when he came home, the voice of the woman he met in the forest would not leave his head since he could not share what he saw with anybody, including his twin brother; so, one day, he decided to go and dig a hole in the ground and say the words into the ground and get it out of his head that way. So, he dug the hole and said into the hole, I met a woman in the forest with two heads, and she was feeding them, and each one was saying, "It is my turn, It is my turn." Then he covered the hole and left.

After many weeks some little flowers like tubes that children play like flutes started growing all over the hole. It was not long before the children in the village went and collected the tube flowers and started playing with them and using them as flutes; the song that came out went like this: I went deep in the forest and met a woman with two heads, and she was feeding them, and each one was saying, "It is my turn, it is my turn!"

In a very short time, the whole village started talking about the song the children were playing with their flutes, and the words spread all over to other towns, and people started asking questions about the terms and what they meant. The rumors spread like fire, and soon the woman in the forest heard it and knew where it came from. She was very annoyed that Kobina Ata Kakra lied to her and decided to take vengeance on him.

So, she turned herself into a beautiful young woman and came to the village; everyone admired her beauty, and soon most of the men were attracted to her. She challenged the men in the town that anyone who could shoot an arrow straight into the center of the board would become her husband. You can imagine how the men flocked into the contest area to try their luck, but no one succeeded. It was almost a shame on the town's men until someone said, It was unfortunate that the twins were not there, especially Kobina Ata Kakra, because he would have hit the center of the board with his first shot.

So, people asked where the twins were, and someone went to Kobina Ata Kakra's house, and he was sleeping. They awakened him and told him about the challenge and how everyone had failed. So it was up to him to save the town's men from shame. He got up and went to take the challenge, and sure enough, he shot just one arrow, and it went right in the center; everyone shouted for joy, and Kakra had a wife, and the celebration was grand.

When the night came, the couple slept in Kakra's room, next to his mother's bedroom. The mother was a wise woman and was not very happy about her son's marriage to a woman he hardly knew. So she was not sleeping when the couple started sharing about their lives. The wife was asking questions that prompted the mother-in-law's ears to perk up, and she stayed very alert and listened to the conversation with great interest. It was a good thing that she was listening because the woman was asking Kakra where he got his powers and why no one but him was able to hit the center of the target; when he answered that, the woman kept asking more and more personal questions and Kakra was just telling her everything. When he said that he had only one last and final answer to give about his powers and was about to say it, his mother shouted at him: How foolish can you be telling all your secrets to a woman in one night? The word he was going to say began with the letter "B," so he did not finish what it was, no matter how the woman bugged him after that.

At daybreak, Kakra's mother lectured him about what he had done: he had exposed himself to a new wife when he knew nothing about her background except the little that she had shared with him and that he only got to her through a challenge of competition and who knows why she was so interested in learning all about his gifts and powers and what he could do. Did he ever think about what she could use those answers for soon? Kakra was sorry and thanked his mother for interrupting him before he could share the whole word of his last gift with his new wife. To a wise woman, that was a warning or a red flag because nobody with good intentions will want to know everything about her husband's gifts in one night, even though she may be surprised at how he just shot one arrow that went straight to the center of the board.

The woman stayed for a couple of weeks, and after her stay in the village, she asked Kakra that they go and visit her parents. And so a time was set, and they prepared to meet and greet her family. Several people came to see them off the morning they were leaving, and they took the bush path to go to her village, but she soon turned to another way and took them deep into the forest. Soon Kakra realized what had happened since he remembered some of the areas they traveled as the same road he took a couple of years ago to where the woman with two heads lived. Yet, he followed her for a long time to see what would happen and if he remembered correctly about the road.

When they had finally gone very deep into the forest, the woman turned and faced him and said, Kobina Ata Kakra, when you visited me here some years ago and when I asked you what you saw, you told me you did not see anything. I told you then that I would come and find you if you had seen me and went out to say anything to the world. And now you must tell me how my story became a song in the world? Kakra knew he was in trouble, so he immediately changed into a bird and flew away, and she changed into another bird that could kill Kakra. And so it went from one gift of change into another, and since he had shared almost everything with her, she would always change into something more powerful to destroy him. All this time, he was heading back home to his village as fast as possible with every change he made.

At the village, his twin brother Kobina Ata Penyin felt something wrong was happening with his brother, so he took his bow and arrows, plus a gun, and rode his horse toward the road his brother had taken with his wife. Not long before Penyin arrived, Kakra had reached the same place on the outskirts of the village and had changed into the toilet (excrement) behind one of the houses. The woman pursuing him had also transformed into a giant dog and wondered what that "B" word was. In our language, the toilet is called "bin," which begins with a "B;" the same applies to the Ghanaian terms for stone, plantain, and cassava—all these words start with a "B." Bankye is cassava, bronze is plantain and boba is stone; it just so happened that all of those things were lying around the place the dog was wandering, trying to sniff out which one was the one Kakra had changed into when suddenly Penyin arrived at the site and saw this vast dog panting and looking around.

He knew right away that the dog was not good and took his gun out, and immediately the dog jumped to attack him, and *bang* went the gun, and the dog was killed instantly. As soon as Penyin had killed the woman in the form of a giant dog, Kakra changed back into his human form and embraced his brother, thanking him for saving his life as usual, because we all know that dogs eat toilet and would finally have chosen to eat the bathroom since it could not eat any of the other things there beginning with the letter "B."

The twin brothers went home, and Kakra told Penyin what he had been through. If it had not been for their mother, he would have died before Penyin even got there to save his life. After hearing everything his brother had to say, Penyin told him to go and tell their mother what he had been through. He was only alive because of her interruption into their conversation the first night the woman was with Kakra. Penyin offered to go with his twin to their mother, so Kakra could share what he had been through that day before Penyin rescued him at the last second of his life. So, they both went and shared with their mother what had happened, and their mother was more than happy that her two sons were still alive since the dog tried to attack Penyin as well. After that experience, Kobina Ata Kakra was careful whom he shared his God-given gifts with. So, stories like this will be told to children so they will learn how not to talk about what they have learned from their families with outside people and know what to share and what not to share, especially with strangers. The wise sayings and proverbs that will go with such stories will be:

Experience is the best teacher.

A hairstyle that a child is demanding must be cut and styled by the parent and shown to them.

A parent's discipline will never kill their child.

A case that will be settled peacefully always has a good intervener.

If you do not stop involving yourself in problems, you will not also have peace.

Don't trouble, trouble, till the situation troubles you!

You don't try to frighten a fire when you are too brave!

A frog's length is only seen when it is dead!

ADDITIONAL PROVERBS AND WISE SAYINGS

Because the tortoise has no family, it carries its coffin everywhere.
(One must be prepared if one knows they do not have relatives to depend upon in time of need.)

A bird that will not fare well in life always builds its nest on the wayside.
(A person who never wants to become anything in life always finds excuses not to work or study.)

A child that will not let her mother sleep will also not sleep.
(If you will not stop involving yourself in problems, you will also not have peace.)

A child that learns how to wash their hands well will eat with adults.
(If you respect yourself, you get invited to important meetings at a very young age.)

Double slaps make one dizzy!
(One does not have to tackle two difficult tasks at the same time.)

A fowl's feet do not kill its chicks.
(A parent's discipline will never kill their child.)

When mouth meets mouth, there is no conflict.
(When people take time to communicate with each other, it clears confusion.)

The ear does not judge in favor of a brother or sister.
(One does not only tell the truth when it affects a family member.)

The animal that will have a clean hide is the one that receives the bullet shot in the head.
(A case that will be settled peacefully always has a good intervener.)

If a child is responsive to the needs of others, they enjoy what they like best.
(A kind person enjoys favors from others.)

Necessity carries one far away.

(Being poor or unable to fend for yourself will take you to places you do not want to go.)

Necessity is the mother of invention.

(When you are desperate, you can be creative.)

The Devil naturally lodges with the Witch when as a stranger in a town.

(When a problematic person travels, they end up with another problematic person in town.)

Though Asam and Asansam are rhyming in name, they are different creatures.

(We may have the same name, but we do not have the same character. Or we may come from the same family but have quite different characters.)

Falsity, hatred, and disagreement always draw the Devil nearer.

(Discontent and hatred create disharmony.)

Patience is bitter, but its fruit is sweet.

(Taking time to do something is often frustrating, but when you finish with it and look at what you have done, you feel content.)

A mirror is of no use to the blind person.

(If you have any help to offer somebody, do not wait until they cannot make use of it.)

A bird's sister or brother is the one that sleeps in the same nest.

(One's neighbor is the one who knows their needs.)

A wound given by a word is more complicated to cure than that provided by a sword.

(It is easier to heal a wound from a beating than a wound from disgrace.)

If the palm tree is considered dangerous, then it is because of its thorny branches.

(People are only afraid of those in authority because they have laws on their side.)

The warrior unit that has never gone to battle before has no oath to swear.

(Without a personal involvement or experience of any event, one has nothing to compare a new event or problem with.)

Each new day has its own problems.

(One cannot depend upon bygone days for survival.)

When one has presented salt as a gift, that person should not receive pepper in return!

(When one offers you kindness, you do not offer wickedness in return for their service.)

"Atofamber," the red herbaceous plant, grows with its color from the seed.

(One is born with intelligence. Or one does not inherit intelligence.)

One sees the true length of the frog when it is dead!

(One sees a person's true nature when a difficult situation arises. A person's true character comes out when they are under stress or pressure.)

When meat is abundant, the wolf's toothache is most painful.

(One loses the power of speech when the occasion demands it. Or sometimes, a person does not rise to the standard when the event requires it.)

Some years are full of misfortunes.

(There are times when one can never do anything right. Or, no matter what you do, there are occasions in life when nothing seems possible.)

A child learns to crack a snail's shell but not that of a tortoise!
(One must learn to take on what one can adequately handle. Or no matter how strong you are, you must not fight a dozen people all by yourself.)

If a child has a big mouth, they learn to eat behind the river, but they must not use it for a ferryboat.
(When someone knows how to gossip, they must do so closer to home but not try to do that in a place where they would get into trouble.)

(Another interpretation would be: If one knows how to meddle in other people's affairs, they must do so closer to home and not try to do so in a foreign country.)

ACKNOWLEDGMENTS

The author is deeply indebted to the Order of Saint Helena, the African Brothers of the Order of the Holy Cross, and several people without whose encouragement this book would not have been written and published.

I wish to express my gratitude above all, to my father and mother, Kobina Foh (Mr. S. K. Ampah) and Esi Egyiribah (Christina Merful-Ampah), for raising me with love and giving me a sense of self-confidence that has endured and flowed throughout the course of a whole life dedicated to God's service.

My gratitude extends to the late Archbishop of the Province of West Africa, the Most Rev. I. S. LeMaire, and his wife, Mrs. Hannah LeMaire, for their caring role in my childhood and upbringing. My gratitude goes to my stepmother, Monica Hagan, who raised me from an impossible teenager to a wonderful and loving adult!

I am also indebted to the Rev. Dr. Dale T. Irvin, Professor of Theology at New York Theological Seminary. To the late Rev. Vincent Shamo, a priest in charge of St. Mary the Virgin Anglican Church in Accra, Ghana, West Africa, who first encouraged me to write down these proverbs after becoming aware of my skills in using proverbs whenever I spoke and told stories.

My special thanks go to the late Mr. Robert Wynn and his wife, Mrs. Wilhelmina Wynn. Mrs. Wynn gave endless time and energy to the process of recording these proverbs by reading and rereading the stories and asking questions. Her questions led to more proverbs being recalled from memory.

I am very grateful to the Order of Saint Helena and all of the sisters, both past and present, and especially to the members of my present household in North Augusta, South Carolina. They have encouraged me to publish the rest of the stories that Yellow Moon Publication did not publish. I also wish to acknowledge Rev. Sr. Ellen Francis, OSH, who edited the contract, and Sr. Ann Prentice, OSH, who proofread and edited the book's first printing. Both sisters dedicated their love, skills, and hours to compiling and proofing this unique collection of Ghanaian proverbs.

To my family in Ghana, who graciously helped to edit the proverbs already written and added some new ones I had forgotten, I say a big Thank You!

Reverend Canon Rosina Ampah, OSH

Order of Saint Helena

ABOUT THE AUTHOR

The Rev. Sister Rosina A. Ampah first received a call to religious life as a little girl when she was nearly five years old. The story is that in her homeland of Ghana, West Africa, she entered a church early one morning when someone called out to her. They asked her to come before the altar, where she heard these words uttered, "God said to tell you that you will become an Anglican priest."

She ran to tell the local priest that God had told her she would one day become a priest. The local priest kindly replied that women were not allowed to be ordained as priests in the Anglican Communion or Roman Catholic Church. This did not dissuade or deter Rosina.

Many years later, she came to the Order of Saint Helena to dedicate herself to God's service in whatever way she could. As a member of OSH, she has been able to respond to her original calling, serving now as both a Sister of the Order and as an Episcopal priest.

In 1993 Sister Rosina became the first Ghanaian-Anglican woman in The Episcopal Church to be ordained to the priesthood and, in 2004, the first woman to be made a Canon in the Anglican Diocese of Cape Coast, Ghana, West Africa. Her days are filled with prayer, service, and life within this religious community.

NOTES

 Gye Nyame is an Adinkra symbol that means "Except God." It conveys the omnipotence and supremacy of God in all relationships within and across creation. Adinkra symbols from Ghana represent cultural concepts, traditional wisdom, and facets of life or the environment often linked with proverbs.

Gye Nyame is one of the most widespread Adinkra symbols expressing the deep faith Akans have in the Supreme Being, Onyame (Nyame), Onyankopɔn, Twereduampɔn (the reliable one), and other meanings. It captures the faith of an African people who see God's involvement in every aspect of human life. In the Akan cosmology, God (Nyame) is omnipotent, omnipresent, and omniscient.

Ghanaian proverbs have a long history going back many generations, even centuries. One of the missions of this book is to preserve the original and historical context in which each story arose. To do so, they are being presented as the stories were passed down from one generation to the next in an oral tradition.

We urge the reader to keep this in mind whenever a conflict may appear with today's values in the 21st Century. Embedded within this rich oral tradition spanning multiple generations, a profound cultural heritage is present and accessible, especially when viewed through a lens of diversity and tolerance.

We ask the reader to look past any such conflicts and seek out the inherent and folkloric wisdom held and treasured within these stories.

Book Cover & Interior
Type Settings & Fonts:

Lane Narrow
Lane Humouresque
PERPETUA TILTING MT
GARAMOND — Garamond